Sherlock Holmes and The Unmasking of the Whitechapel Horror

Frank Emerson

Paperback ISBN 978-1-80424-169-1
ePub ISBN 978-1-80424-170-7
PDF ISBN 978-1-80424-171-4

Published by MX Publishing
335 Princess Park Manor, Royal Drive,
London, N11 3GX
www.mxpublishing.co.uk

Cover design Brian Belanger

An Exordium for the Reader

Prior to your embarkation on the story that follows, I feel duty-bound to offer some sort of explanatory introduction. The adventure is easily one of the longest and most convoluted among those singular undertakings that have made up the nearly thirty-five year career which I shared with my best friend, Mr. Sherlock Holmes.

As you are doubtless aware, many of the activities of Jack the Ripper and those of Sherlock Holmes occurred within the same time period and indeed within the same geographic area.

One may be under the impression that Holmes never addressed the unspeakable acts of the Whitechapel horror. This is incorrect. Although it is true that Holmes' efforts in this matter have never been expounded upon by me or any other would-be reporter that is not to say that they did not exist. Quite the contrary. Holmes was involved with the investigation into the fiend's activities from the very beginning to the end, which he was most instrumental in bringing about, some fifteen years later.

It has taken me a considerable length of time to accurately amass the facts of the saga so that I might put them into a coherent form and publish them in a public forum. The end result is what you are about to read. In an effort to set the scene for you, I have begun the story with a number of prelusive sentences, which illustrate how and why this chronicle came about.

-- John H. Watson, MD
Baker Street, Marylebone
Westminster, London
1920

Part I

Chapter One

I am writing this on the 8th of April in the year 1920 from the comfort of my home at 221B Baker Street, to where my late wife and I had moved from our lodging in Queen Anne Street in 1908. As I reflect on the many and varied adventures I have shared with my dear friend, Mr. Sherlock Holmes, my reveries take me back to another 8th of April, some seventeen years past. It was on that occasion that Holmes and I, together with our colleague, former Detective Chief Inspector Frederick Abberline of Scotland Yard, had spent the preceding afternoon, evening and this morning in animated discussion. The topic of that discussion was our involvement in the horrifying events of the prior fifteen years, which achieved its culmination in the proceedings of the previous morning.

To begin at the beginning then, it was mid-morning on the 7th of April, 1903, and we had just returned from Wandsworth Prison in South West London, where we had been invited to witness the execution of Severin Klosowski, also known as George Chapman, but whom the world had come to know as Jack the Ripper. The disagreeable nature of the penetrating, chilly, almost threatening drizzle was an appropriate reflection of the character of the monster whose well-deserved fate we had come to observe. We were fairly expressionless as we stood with Major Knox, the governor of the prison, in the small, white-washed death chamber and watched as Mr. William Billington, the executioner, enabled

1

this human abomination to plunge through the trap door of the gallows on his six foot-six inch journey to hell.

It is worth noting that DCI Abberline had been the one to draw us into the horrifying miasma of the Whitechapel murders in the autumn of 1888. Through the conduct of a cooperative investigation and by dint of persevering detective work, Holmes and he, with my assistance, had been able to deduce that the horrors had continued, perpetrated by the same man, with some irregularity until 1901 in America as well as England. Therefore it was altogether fitting that the three of us should together attend the fulfillment of our efforts.

Following the event, we did not linger as the deceased was allowed to swing beneath the gallows for the required one hour, to ensure that the sentence had been carried out. We looked on that practice as an antiquated and quaint formality. We were quite certain he was dead.

As we passed from the execution shed and out through the prison gate, we could not help but notice what can only be described as a tableau of singular oddity. Standing a short distance from the shed, a crowd had collected, which consisted of a goodly number of journalists, police officials, and no few curious citizens, and which roared in approval as the black flag was hoisted above the prison wall. Further on, supported by the arm of her brother-in-law, Stanislas, and attended by her sister, Alice, was the quietly sobbing Lucy Klosowski, the widow of the dead man. Though we had interviewed her in the past, we thought it best to allow her some semblance of privacy at this time to reflect on what must have been a flood of confusing, contradictory thoughts whirling in her brain about the fiend who had been in fact, the father of her two children.

Thus, in an attitude of bittersweet satisfaction, we entered our growler, which we had previously requisitioned for the morning, for a pleasant enough hour and a half trip back to Marylebone, whereupon we adjourned to the fireside of Holmes's Baker Street rooms.

Over several warming brandies, Holmes and Abberline also indulging in cigars, the conversation covered all areas of our long association as we had sought to apprehend the perpetrator of the Ripper murders, and our ensuing efforts to solve the mystery that had bedeviled the police forces of two countries for the past fifteen years. Eventually, I took my leave to return to Queen Anne Street while Abberline was to spend the night at Baker Street and return to his home in Bournemouth by train the following morning.

Fortunately, I had been mindful enough to take extensive notes during the conversation. Relying upon them, and my own memories of the developments of the crimes and notes made during the inquiries and investigations, I shall endeavor to provide a true and accurate deposition of this singular case.

To begin with then, it was not an unseasonable early evening on September 13th, 1888, as Sherlock Holmes and I sat in the parlour of 221B Baker Street discussing our latest adventure involving a Greek interpreter and two miscreants named Kemp and Latimer. Dissatisfied that the adventure had played out without appropriate justice, Holmes was expounding on his suspicion that the entire affair bore the acrid scent of the involvement of Professor James Moriarty, whom he described as the "Napoleon of Crime."

We were interrupted when Mrs. Hudson knocked at the door to announce that we had two gentleman visitors, an event which was somewhat untoward at this hour of the day. Nonetheless, we asked her to show them in. Leading the way was our most recent official police companion, the tall, tow-headed Inspector Tobias Gregson of Scotland Yard. He was accompanied by a rather sturdy individual, whose bushy side whiskers only served to accentuate the scarcity of hair on his head.

Before introductions could be made, Holmes took the offensive. "Hello Gregson! Watson and I were just discussing our latest adventure with you and how the last act, so to speak, seemed to be unfulfilled. Have you made any progress as to the whereabouts of Kemp and Latimer and their traveling companion? And is there any hint of Professor Moriarty?"

"Er, no, Mr. Holmes," said Gregson, somewhat taken aback at Holmes's preemptive questioning. "Though there is nothing concrete, through channels we've learned that they may have made their way to the Continent and we have dispatched agents to investigate the rumor, but in truth, I do not hold out much hope for resolution. As to Moriarty, we have heard even less."

"Hmm, yes. Just as I suspected would be the case regarding the professor," sighed Holmes.

"To the point of my visit then, Mr. Holmes: this is..."

"No need, Gregson. Even a blind man would recognize DCI Abberline from the pictures in *The Illustrated Police*

News," Holmes said as he stepped forward to shake the inspector's hand. "Allow me to introduce my friend and colleague, Dr. John Watson."

The inspector shook my hand and complimented me on my work with Holmes.

"Now then," Holmes continued, "I must say, Chief Inspector, it is really no test of my deductive abilities to discern why you've come here. My only question is why you've taken so long in seeking my assistance in the matter which is the talk of all London and beyond, to wit: the recent barbarous murders in Whitechapel."

"You are of course correct, Mr. Holmes. As to why you have not been approached up until to this point, I have no excuse save that Sir Charles Warren, the Commissioner of Police, has determined that the professional efforts of Scotland Yard are of sufficient expertise to resolve the matter and bring the perpetrator to justice."

"I see," said Holmes as he crossed to the mantelpiece, retrieved the Persian slipper that served as his tobacco hamper, filled his pipe and proceeded to light it. Ending the pause that ensued, he asked, "Watson, would you mind offering our guests some brandy? Chief Inspector? Gregson?"

Being anxious to follow where I sensed the conversation might be going, I complied. Gregson begged off with the excuse that he had been present only to expedite the introduction and that a pressing engagement at Metropolitan Police Headquarters demanded his attention. With a nod around, he took his leave. DCI Abberline seemed somewhat relieved at the invitation, accepted the brandy and at my suggestion, seated himself on the sofa. Holmes and I, brandies in hand, took seats on side chairs opposite him across a low table.

"If it is not impertinent on my part, Chief Inspector, will you tell us how many professionals Sir Charles has assigned to these murders?"

The chief inspector gave a nervous cough. "There are twenty-three detectives, two clerks, one inspector, which is myself, and numerous constables."

"And how far along have you got in your efforts?" asked Holmes, not in an unkind manner, for he knew the difficulties involved in such an investigation.

"If I may speak directly, Sir Charles is a fine man and has had an admirable and successful career in the military, but he is not a policeman. Though his efforts are well-meaning, I fear that his capabilities and methods are limited by his lack of appropriate experience and coloured by unintended prejudice against non-professional investigations in which category, I am sorry to say, he has included you. That is why I asked Gregson for an introduction, so that I might come to you on my own, to correct Sir Charles's oversight, in the hope that we might join forces to solve the murders and bring this monster to justice, Mr. Holmes"

Holmes stood abruptly, raised his snifter of brandy and with a determined smile said, "There is nothing neither Watson nor I would like better than to be of assistance in this investigation. Since we are now colleagues, I suggest that we dispense with formality. We are Holmes and Watson and you are Abberline. Is that agreeable to you?"

Abberline let out a breath, raised his glass and said, "Eminently agreeable, Holmes. Eminently agreeable. Now as you know, we have two horrible murders that we assume are related: Polly Nichols on the 31st of August and Annie Chapman on the 8th of this month."

"I am sorry to interrupt you, Abberline," said Holmes, "but I fear you may be somewhat in error."

"Oh, how so?"

"Correct me if I am wrong, but I am certain that I am not, but wasn't there an earlier murder of another drab, named Martha Tabram, in the same vicinity who was done away with in a similar manner?"

"Yes, of course."

"Why is she not included in your victim tally?"

"Two reasons: firstly, unlike the other two, she was murdered on a weeknight. Secondly, she was stabbed thirty-nine times, more than the other two victims combined."

"Let me ask you, Abberline, were all of the wounds inflicted upon Mrs. Tabram delivered with the same weapon?"

"Why no, they were not, but how did you know that?"

"Judging by the way the wounds were described in the newspaper, I concluded that the wound to the throat was administered with a short-bladed knife, while the others bore the indications of a longer blade being used – particularly the wound piercing her heart. This bears a marked resemblance to the weapon that was determined to have been employed in the murders of Mrs. Nichols and Mrs. Chapman. That tells me that not only were two weapons involved, but perhaps two murderers. It is my contention that the fiend you are seeking did indeed murder Nichols and Chapman but was perhaps a late-comer to the Tabram murder.

"Her throat had been slashed and she was lying in George Yard, most likely in the process of dying. The suspect came upon her there in his quest for a victim. The original assailant being scared away, he then stabbed her through the heart to prevent further bleeding, and proceeded to inflict the subsequent wounds upon her, in what could only be described as a frenzy – most likely brought on by a deviant sexual urge, such as that which I believe is evidenced in the following murders. I should also note that to judge from the description of the pools of blood close in around the victims: Mrs. Nichols and Mrs. Chapman, were strangled first to stop the heart from pumping. That would eliminate the possibility of the murderer being covered with blood, which would have undoubtedly been the case, had the heart continued to pump."

"The manner of death makes perfect sense, but really, Holmes," Abberline exclaimed as he abruptly rose from the sofa, "a sexual frenzy? That is ridiculous! I don't see it, I just don't see it at all! Surely, Holmes, such an aberration cannot truly exist?"

"Oh yes, my dear Abberline, it can and does. Tell me: did you consider robbery as being a motive in the slayings? No, of course you didn't. Witness testimonies as to earlier events of the evenings in question tend to corroborate each other in the fact that the women were, as they say, skint. Having exhausted what meagre funds they had on drink, they were desperate to secure money for a night's shelter – at one of the numerous doss houses in the vicinity – which they were each attempting to do by way of plying their trade. That eliminates the motive of robbery.

"One of the tenets of my methods is that once you eliminate the impossible, whatever remains, no matter how improbable, must be the truth. To further apply a favourite precept of mine, which I have borrowed from Herr Arthur Schopenhauer and which you have just now eminently demonstrated, all truth passes through three stages. First, it is ridiculed. Second, it is violently opposed. Third, it is accepted as being self-evident. There being nothing left of possible motives, the expression of emotion, as violent and morbidly aberrant as it may be, must be it.

"As to the existence of such a perversion, Dr. Richard von Krafft-Ebing, in his recent work *Psychopathia Sexualis*, has identified the existence of such a perversion as a very real thing, being a combination of cerebral neurosis, not the least of which are sadism, necrophilia and satyriasis, all of which point to the behaviour of our as-yet-unknown killer."

"My word, Holmes, you amaze me," said Abberline, to which I added my agreement.

Holmes gave a short laugh as Abberline re-seated himself on the sofa. "Surely you didn't think I would restrict my reading to melittology texts and *The Police Gazette*? Watson will agree with me that education never ends." I nodded. "Further, I believe said precept is no more applicable than in the profession of consulting detective. Watson, please do the honours once more, would you?"

I was more than happy to comply, as I believed that this demonstration of Holmes's unique erudition called for another drink.

"Now," said Holmes, "where were we? Have your investigations yielded any likely suspects?"

"You must understand, Holmes," Abberline answered, "that we have not been alone in the conduct of our investigations. Contrary to Sir Charles's wishes, a number of citizens of the area have formed an ad hoc organisation calling itself the Whitechapel Vigilance Committee with a Mr. George Lusk, an interior decorator by trade, to be its chairman. Even though my men have canvassed the area and conducted extensive interviews with the locals, this group of vigilantes has grown impatient with our efforts and has taken it upon itself to make inquiries that have done nothing to help our search and in fact have done much to hinder our progress by intimidating potential witnesses and suspects.

"Despite this, by studying the nature of the crimes, we have been able to develop a number of theories about the perpetrator, which have led us to several candidates, shall we say, for the position of fiend."

"Capital," said Holmes, "please enlighten us."

"Even taking into consideration Mrs. Tabram, which I had not done until your analysis just now, by the features of the attacks, we have surmised that the individual has some knowledge of surgical techniques and anatomy. So he – and we are most certain that these crimes were committed by a man – maybe a physician. We are also working under the very likely supposition that the man is not a stranger to the area and probably resides nearby."

"Excellent," said Holmes. "I agree with you that the killer is undoubtedly male, not just from the viciousness of the attacks, but the fact that he is consorting with drabs in such a place and at such an hour. However, if the individual is a denizen of the area, which I believe to be the case, it is highly unlikely that someone of the social standing of a physician or a surgeon would select such an impoverished district in which to reside. It is more likely that the man has had some surgical training, perhaps as an apprentice, nurse or doctor's assistant or even a barber. As you are doubtless aware, barbers, particularly in the poorer areas, are often called upon to perform minor surgeries. With these factors in mind, can you still offer up any potential malefactors?"

"Yes, I believe I can, Holmes, although the evidence we have been able to gather is flimsy to say the least and since there was no cause to detain the suspects on this account, they remain at large but under observation.

"The first possibility is one Thomas Cutbush, a clerk by trade but with an intense interest in medical texts which, according to his employer, he pores over whenever possible. He is known to frequent Whitechapel in the company of prostitutes, one or more of whom infected him with syphilis some years back. He has spent time in the Lambeth Asylum for the insane, during which period he often mentioned his abiding animosity toward ladies of the evening.

"Hmm," said Holmes as he puffed on his oily Peterson. "Next?"

"Aaron Kosminski is a Polish Jew who resides in Whitechapel and is employed as a hairdresser or a barber in Greenfield Street. He has been interned several times at the Mile End Old Town Workhouse due to the unstable nature of his sanity, which was brought on, according to records of the asylum by untreated venereal disease. My colleague Chief Inspector Donald Swanson favours Kosminski as the prime suspect."

"Whitechapel, of course, is home to many immigrant Jews, so Kosminski's religion would not come into play, I believe," said Holmes. "The relevant facts are his occupation and mental condition. Please continue, Abberline."

"One Francis Thompson meets most of the requirements you've set forth. He is one of those residents we questioned in hopes that he might have been a witness to any unusual circumstances, but the more he was questioned, the more he was to come under suspicion. Inquiries of his family uncovered the information that he was the son of a doctor and that he himself had been in medical school.

"These past three years he had been living in poverty conditions in Spitalfields, during which time he attempted to earn a living as a writer and poet. During this time also, he became addicted to opium. Being a strong Catholic, to the extremes I should call it, he often wrote of his severe disdain of the immorality of prostitutes. During questioning, it was discovered that he often carried a dissecting knife on his person under his coat. All of this would seem to put him in the forefront of the suspects."

"So it would seem," said Holmes. "Have you any others?"

"There are a number of others, Holmes, and doubtless more will surface as the investigation"...

"And the killings," Homes inserted.

"...continue. Yes, Holmes. I fear you might be right. However there is one other individual in whom I've taken a personal interest, and he also meets your criteria. His name is Severin Klosowski, and he is a Polish immigrant having arrived here in March of last year. His record states that he trained extensively in Poland as a junior surgeon, which attests to the fact that in Poland, he was qualified to practice. As he found, doubtless to his dismay, this qualification was not reciprocal in England. Mr. Klosowski was only able to secure a position as a hairdresser's assistant. After some months, he opened a barbershop at 126 Cable Street, where he also now resides.

"Following an initial interview by a constable, who stated that Klosowski seemed quite unnerved by the process, I then took it upon myself to interview him further at Metropolitan Police headquarters. He was polite, yet terse. He seemed less unnerved and more put out, with an underlying layer of restrained anger.

"I questioned a number of Klosowski's neighbours. Although couching their testimonies in reluctance, they for the most part concurred that while Klosowski was generally polite, he did possess a temper, which he would sometimes display at odd moments. A number of them said that they had seen him in various pubs in the area and that after he had taken drink, his temper would flare at whomever he was talking with at the time – man or woman. It's interesting, Holmes. I felt that if there was one common, overriding attitude among the neighbours as I questioned them, it was one of extreme caution – not toward me mind you, but toward Klosowski."

"I see," said Holmes. "I find myself in agreement with your analysis, Abberline. Though the others you have named are somewhat intriguing, I believe that Mr, Klosowski may be the answer. His history, as you have described it, indicates that he is in possession of an intellect clearly superior to the other suspects. He is familiar with surgical techniques and he is of a somewhat unstable temperament that he is at pains to control."

"What do you suggest I do, Holmes?"

"It seems to me that at the moment, you can do nothing more than what you are doing, save increasing the police presence in Whitechapel and continuing the interviews with the citizenry. Please do not hesitate to contact me if you find that I might be of any further assistance, though I fear at this point, you are conducting the manhunt much as I would. I am truly sorry that I cannot be of more help to you at present."

"Very well, Holmes," said Abberline as he stood and made his way to the door. "Thank you for your advice. You may be assured that I will be calling on you again as this series of hideous events plays itself out. Good evening to you both. I'll show myself out"

"Well Holmes" I said once Abberline had left, "what do you make of this?"

"What do I make of it? What I make of it is that Scotland Yard is doing its utmost, which will probably not be sufficient without our help. Abberline was very wise in seeking us out – we must remember to thank Gregson on the matter – but I am quite certain, unfortunately, that he will again seek our counsel before much longer, unless I am wrong, which of course I am not."

A fortnight had passed before we again heard from Abberline and the continued Whitechapel atrocities. In the meantime, Holmes and I had become involved with the case of the insidious Thaddeus Sholto, from which the only fortunate result, and I believe to be my saving grace, was my introduction to Miss Mary Morstan, who agreed to become my wife. I must say that Holmes, despite his affection for me as a partner and friend, did not react favourably to my engagement because of his belief that he sees rationality, which is the bedrock of deductive reasoning, as being totally incompatible with emotion.

In what I can only describe as an almost childlike reaction to my good fortune, he again took up the syringe of a seven-percent cocaine solution, to which he turned when confronted with certain problems or an extended period of inactivity. I had been striving to wean him from this unnecessary dependency, but had met with uneven success. Thus it was that I was relieved when we again heard from Abberline which served to redirect Holmes' attention from the needle back to the affair to which he had previously begun to apply his skills.

Part One
Chapter Two

It was the afternoon of September 29th, Holmes and I had just returned to Baker Street following a pleasant midday meal at The Beehive in Crawford Street. As we rounded the corner, we were met by the agitated figure of DCI Abberline.

"Holmes! Watson!" he cried. "Thank heaven you're here! Mrs. Hudson invited me to wait inside for you, but I was too nervous and was about to go on a search, but now here you are."

"There, there, Abberline," I said, "you've obviously worked yourself into quite a state. I insist that you come in, perhaps have a small whisky to help you calm yourself and let us know how we can be of service." Holmes opened the door and we all went in and up the stairs.

Abberline could barely restrain himself as we entered the parlour. I crossed to the sideboard and poured three small whiskies, two of which I delivered to Holmes and Abberline. The inspector downed his straight away and then fumbled in his pocket from which he withdrew a folded piece of paper.

"Here," he said as he unfolded the paper. "This letter arrived at Scotland Yard just this afternoon, by way of the Central News Office." He spread the letter open for us to read the following:

Dear Boss,

I keep on hearing the police have caught me but they wont fix me just yet. I have laughed when they look so clever and talk about being on the right track. That joke about

Leather Apron gave me real fits. I am down on whores and I shant quit ripping them till I do get buckled. Grand work the last job was. I gave the lady no time to squeal.

How can they catch me now. I love my work and want to start again. You will soon hear of me with my funny little games. I saved some of the proper red stuff in a ginger beer bottle over the last job to write with but it went thick like glue and I cant use it. Red ink is fit enough I hope ha ha. The next job I do I shall clip the lady's ears off and send to the police officers just for jolly wouldn't you. Keep this letter back till I do a bit more work, then give it out straight.

My knife's so nice and sharp I want to get to work right away if I get a chance.

Good Luck.

Yours truly

Jack the Ripper

Dont mind me giving the trade name. Wasnt good enough to post this before I got all the red ink off my hands curse it No luck yet. They say I'm a doctor now. ha ha.

"This is fascinating," said Holmes. "It would seem to me that, by way of the syntax and the penmanship, whoever wrote this was certainly not uneducated. The reference to the Leather Apron accusation indicates that he is fully familiar with your investigation and that it is intended to be a taunt. Further, that this note was first sent to the Central News Office attests to the fact that although he operates in the shadows, he is far from adverse to publicity, in fact that he prefers it. Were it otherwise, Scotland Yard would have been the primary recipient. The mocking, challenging tone of the letter indicates that the writer sees himself in control and in a position of power, which of course is evidenced by the nature of the murders themselves. His desire for fame or notoriety is without fear of apprehension, but that he pursues it, is evidenced by the fact that he gives himself the name, or rather anoints himself with the title, 'Jack the Ripper'"

"Well," said Abberline, "that should certainly be of great interest to Sir Charles. Of course you understand that I cannot let it be known that this analysis comes from a non-professional."

"Certainly, Abberline. Feel free to place the credit for the analysis to where it can be most effectively applied. The important thing is that the deductions can be of help in apprehending the fiend and putting an end to the atrocities. My advice to you is to continue with and perhaps to intensify your efforts."

"Thank you Holmes, Watson, for the analysis, advice and understanding," Abberline said as he refolded the letter, picked up his bowler and headed out the door. After he had left, Holmes filled his pipe, lit it and took a seat on the sofa.

"Well, Watson, what do you think?"

"Regarding what?" I asked.

"Regarding Abberline's chances of apprehending the murderer."

"Oh, I don't know, Holmes. You have certainly given him the benefit of your reasoning, which is no doubt accurate. To me, Abberline certainly seems focused and able and inquisitive enough to capitalise on it."

"I wish I had your confidence, Watson. But judging by Sir Charles Warren's stifling attitude and limited deductive abilities, I fear that despite Abberline's best efforts, Scotland Yard may be unable or unwilling to explore more unconventional avenues of investigation."

With that, Holmes retrieved the most recent issues of *The Star, The Police Gazette* and *The Illustrated Police News* and settled back on the sofa to continue his unceasing research into the less savoury activities of society. I took the opportunity to retire to my room and wade into a book I'd recently acquired, *Dangerous Work: A Diary of an Arctic Adventure*, dealing with a young medical student's adventures as a ship's surgeon on an Arctic whaler. I read for a short while and then fell into a comfortable afternoon nap.

It was after dark when I awoke. Returning to the parlour, I found that Holmes had left. I was not to see him again until the following morning.

Part I

Chapter Three

It was very early Sunday morning when I awakened from a fitful sleep, thinking of the murders and fearful of what lay in store. I rose and entered the sitting room. The door to Holmes's bedroom was open, and I could see that his bed had not been slept in. This only increased my concern. Suddenly I heard a clamour and clatter just outside the door to the entryway. The time being just after sunrise, I was nonplussed, as you can understand. Preferring to err on the side of caution, I retrieved my Mark III Adams service revolver from my desk, crossed the room and flung open the door.

To say that I was astonished, does not accurately describe my reaction. What greeted me was a somewhat tall, thin yet stooped old crone with an odour of gin about her and who had, one could only hope, seen better days. From her highly rouged concave cheeks, likewise her cupid bow lips and her blonde poor excuse for a wig that seemed to be trying to escape from under a floppy bonnet, I took her to be a street walker: one whom I could not imagine as meeting with much success in plying her trade. She was writhing about and fumbling beneath her amply draped clothing as if tormented by vermin. I was taken aback. "Look here, my good woman," I said as I regained my senses and gestured with my revolver, "I fear you may have been misdirected in your travels. Now if you will please contain yourself…"

"No, Watson, I believe it is you who should contain yourself and please put that pistol away before you have an accident and shoot me while I am trying to locate my key. Now please step aside and let me in," said the old crone in a voice that could only be that of Sherlock Holmes.

"Holmes! My word, Holmes, I believe you have outdone yourself this time! I tell you, The Theatre Royal is so much the poorer for you having chosen to become the world's first consulting detective."

"The world's *only* consulting detective but never mind that at the moment, Watson," said Holmes brusquely as he pushed by me, placed his Webley Bulldog on the mantelpiece, and made straight for his room.

Ten minutes passed and I had regained my composure, when Holmes stepped back into the room in his long dressing gown. Having visited the facilities, he was still in the process of drying his face after having removed the theatre makeup as he said, "I apologise for my curtness, Watson, but I have had a night's worth of miserable experiences which would have been worth the effort had they produced results, which they most decidedly did not. Not to mind the early hour, I believe I could do with a brandy. Would you do the honours?"

"Of course, Holmes. Now tell me: what have you been at?"

"Suffice it to say, Watson, that earning a living as a streetwalker in Whitechapel is much more difficult than one would imagine. I have spent all night through until this morning incognito, habituating the alleys, nooks and pubs of Whitechapel, even propositioning likely suspects, in hopes of luring out the Ripper or at least gleaning some useful information."

"So were you able to learn anything?"

"Not a thing, Watson. Plus, despite all my endeavours, not only did I not lure out the Ripper, I was unable to attract any suspects, or even any potential customers for that matter, who might have contributed to my investigation. I tell you, Watson, apparently I was not cut out to be a prostitute. If you are to adhere to the honesty of chronicling, you may want to record this as not one of my more shining hours in the field of investigation and deduction," said Holmes as he turned to refill his snifter.

Just then, a knock on our door brought Mrs. Hudson, dressed in her robe and slippers, into the room. Before she could speak, Abberline, with a quick word of apology and thanks to our landlady, launched himself through into the parlour. "Holmes! Watson! I'm afraid I bring very disturbing news. The Ripper struck again last night, only this time with a double murder! We have already been able to identify the victims: The first was one Elizabeth Stride, or 'Long Liz' as she was known in the trade while the second was Catherine Eddowes. Of course both women were bawds. Both had their throats slashed nearly to the spine but curiously enough, only Eddowes was mutilated. There was very little blood at the Stride location, while blood was pooled beneath Eddowes' mutilations"

"I see," said Holmes, "Please calm yourself with a brandy and let us investigate the events in an objective, analytical manner. Now, from what you say, given the nature of the throat slashing as well as that of the pursuant conduct of the blood flow, of course they were both strangled before being subjected to the knife. That fact alone would indicate that they were killed by the same fiend who did the hideous work on the three earlier victims. However, by the difference in the conditions in which these two bodies were found, it would seem that he was not quite finished with Mrs. Stride before he moved on to Mrs. Eddowes. Tell me, where were they found?"

"Mrs. Eddowes body, lying over a coal hole in Mitre Square, Aldgate, was found by PC Edward Watkins. Oddly, she had not been there when he had walked by the place a quarter-hour earlier."

"Quite. And that of Long Liz?"

"Mr. Louis Diemschutz, the steward of the International Working Men's Educational Club in Berner Street, was coming into work early this morning, and when he went out the alley door to see to the trash, he discovered Mrs. Stride just next door in Duffield's Yard," said Abberline.

"My word!" cried Holmes, "I was there! My travels through the area took me along Berner Street. I remember passing by the Educational Club and Duffield's Yard. Of course that was well before Mr. Diemschutz would have been reporting to work. However, I believe my suspicion was correct when I said that the Ripper was not quite finished with his work on Mrs. Stride. I interrupted him! He must have heard me as I made my way down Berner Street and fled through the rear of the alley, whereupon he soon arrived at Mitre Square and paid his unwelcome visit to Catherine Eddowes. Of course I neither heard nor saw anything untoward as Mrs. Stride was already dead and Duffield's Yard is ill lit. If only I had been earlier!"

"Wait, Holmes. Your travels through the area? What do you mean?" asked Abberline.

"My apologies, Abberline, I took it upon myself to don a disguise as a strumpet and venture through Whitechapel in an attempt to lure the monster out. I did not alert you of my plans since you told me of Sir Charles Warren's attitude toward amateurs, such as myself, and did not want to compromise your position. Quite simply: If you had no knowledge of my actions, you could not possibly be held in any blame by way of abetting them."

"I do appreciate that, Holmes, but I must say that your methods, while being quite extraordinary, may be of instructional value to Scotland Yard in the future. You have brought plainclothes investigation to a new level. But there is more you should know with respect to the latest incident."

"Please continue," I said.

Holmes nodded in agreement and Abberline continued, "Following his discovery of Mrs. Eddowes's remains, PC Edwards began to conduct a search of the area. Shortly he came to Goulston Street, where in a recessed doorway, he found a torn section of an apron which was stained with blood and faecal matter and was, in fact, still damp from blood. The apron was determined to have been a piece of one being worn by Catherine Eddowes."

"I see," said Holmes. "It would appear that the Ripper took a piece of the apron to wipe his hands and knife clean of any incriminating evidence and having found a recessed doorway, took the opportunity to be rid of it. No doubt his passion had been sated by his encounter with the unfortunate

Mrs. Eddowes and seeing as how he had nearly been discovered at his labours, his survival instincts took over. The murderer was going to ground as he headed east from Mitre Square."

"That would stand to reason," said Abberline, "as virtually all of our suspects were known to reside deep in the East End of London. But there is one more curious thing to which I must draw your attention.

"On the wall just above where PC Edwards found the piece of apron was written a message in chalk, which may or may not have bearing on the murders."

"Really?" asked Holmes, "and what might that have been?"

Abberline opened his notebook where he had recorded the message. After first reading it aloud, he proffered the page so that we might read the following:

The Juwes are the men that will not be blamed for nothing

Before Holmes could offer his analysis, Abberline explained further, "When he arrived on the scene and read the message, Sir Charles immediately ordered that it be erased. The adjacent area, Petticoat Lane Market, is largely populated by Jewish tradesmen and has been the location of a number of recent anti-Semitic riots. Sir Charles curtly justified his order that the existence of the message would undoubtedly do nothing but stir up more anti-Semitic violence."

"Indeed an interesting theory," said Holmes, "and one which might accomplish Sir Charles's intended purpose, but I fear that it was based on an erroneous assumption. The term

'Juwes' is not a misspelling of the word 'Jews' nor is it an accusation of Jews, though it might indeed be interpreted as such, by the uninitiated or those ignorant of the matter. The term 'Juwe' is integral in the rites and lore of Freemasonry. Tell me, Abberline, is there a Masonic Lodge in the area?"

"Why yes, there is, Holmes. The Masonic Lodge of Joppa is located just at the entrance to Mitre Square."

"I thought there might be," said Holmes. "The message is not anti-Semitic, but rather anti-Masonic, no doubt reflecting someone's personal prejudice or complaint against the Masons in general or the local lodge in particular. Tell me: do you know if Sir Charles is a Mason?"

"As a matter of fact I have noticed that Sir Charles's watch fob bears the Masonic symbol."

"Aha," said Holmes, "all the more reason for Sir Charles to have the message destroyed. But it has absolutely nothing to do with the Ripper. Just think of it Abberline: why would the Ripper foolishly pause in his haste to escape detection by stopping to write such a message? And why would he be carrying chalk?"

"I would think he would not, Holmes. In addition, having seen the actual message before it was eradicated, I can attest that the handwriting bore no resemblance to that of the 'Dear Boss' letter."

"Quite so, Abberline, assuming that letter is authentic. However, I have found that one must never assume anything to be obvious in an investigation, for there is nothing more deceptive than an obvious fact."

"Hmm, yes, I understand, Holmes. But where does that leave us?"

"In a singular fashion, it leaves us slightly ahead of and slightly behind where we were at the onset of these horrors. We are slightly ahead in that you have arrived at a number of suitable suspects. We are behind in that you have not yet been able to apprehend the actual murderer. If I may offer a suggestion, you may want to increase police surveillance in the area and over the suspects you have identified. I should think that this man Klosowski deserves considerable scrutiny."

"Is there nothing else we can do?"

"You might continue to increase your interviews with residents of the area in search of possible witnesses. But mark you, Abberline, take care to understand that residents may provide you with erroneous information based on a prejudice or grudge they might hold against certain other individuals or groups. This would lead to a waste of time on your part and may even aid the fiend in his further endeavours."

Abberline rose, picked up his hat and prepared to leave. "Thank you gentlemen, for your time and advice. I believe that if The Yard takes your analyses into consideration and follows your advice, unaccredited of course, we shall stand a much more reasonable chance of apprehending this beast than we had previously. Thank you both again"

With that, Abberline took his leave. We were left to wonder if he would have any success in tactfully presenting Holmes's theories and suggestions to Sir Charles and if Scotland Yard as a whole would act upon them. It would be over a month before we would hear from Abberline or the Ripper again.

Part I

Chapter Four

For nearly all of October, 1888, our efforts, along with those of Scotland Yard's Inspector Lestrade, were directed toward the devil hound of Baskerville Manor on the Devonshire moors and the insidious and now late and unlamented Jack Stapleton – a sordid affair to say the least.

November found us at loose ends. While I still saw to my few remaining patients, for the most part, I was absorbed with recounting the details of our latest foray, while simultaneously trying to divert Holmes from his seven-per-cent cocaine solution. I arranged for visits to various galleries such as those in Bond Street, concerts and attendance at numerous forensic lectures, with which Holmes was wont to take exception.

It was just after noon of the 10th of November, and Holmes and I had just polished off one of Mrs. Hudson's occasional midday repasts. Holmes was enjoying his first pipe of the day and lamenting the fact that the state of stagnation, in which we temporarily found ourselves, was a cause for his mind to rebel. I surmised that he was referring to the Ripper's activity, or inactivity as it were, when he further opined that this would indeed be a dull world without the presence of lunatics.

As if in answer to Holmes's secular prayer and my not-so-secular pleadings, Mrs. Hudson announced that DCI Abberline, who was just behind her, had once again come calling. As he came through, we noted that his carriage was less frantic than when we had last met, but in his facial expression we read both anger and frustration.

"Abberline, my dear fellow," said Holmes, "you are most welcome, but I fear you are the bearer of news which is none too pleasant."

"Is my misery that obvious?"

"Quite so," I interjected, "perhaps you should have a seat."

"Thank you no, Doctor. At the moment, I prefer to stand."

"Very well then Abberline," said Holmes, "out with it!"

"There has been another murder in Whitechapel, although the word murder is hardly a sufficient name to describe this act of butchery. What befell the unfortunate Mary Jane Kelly is nothing short of obscene. Not only does this mutilation far exceed those of the other victims, but the fact is that it took place in her own flat at 13 Miller's Court off Dorset Street, very near where Annie Chapman was discovered in September."

"Very interesting," said Holmes, "very interesting indeed."

"There is also this, Holmes. Another letter was sent to Mr. George Lusk, chairman of the Whitechapel Vigilance Committee in October, but which he forwarded to Scotland Yard only two days ago."

With that, he produced the letter from his pocket and unfolded it so that we might read the following:

From Hell
Mr Lusk

Sor

> *I send you half the Kidne I took from one woman prasarved it for you tother I fried and ate it was very nise. I may send you the bloody knif that took it out if you only wate a whil longer*
>> *signed*
>> *Catch me when you can Mishter Lusk*

"I am not sure that Mr. Lusk did you any favours by withholding this letter for a month. However, neither am I certain he did you any harm, no matter what his motive – which was undoubtedly his impatience with the Metropolitan Police in their lack of success in the case. Tell me, Abberline, do you happen to have the first letter with you?"

"Certainly, Holmes," said Abberline as he produced it from his pocket.

"Capital," said Holmes as he examined the two side by side. "You can readily see there is no similarity between the handwriting and syntax of the two letters, the second being the work of a much less literate individual. I would state that at least one if not both letters are the work of a charlatan. By any chance did Mr. Lusk include the aforementioned kidney with this latest letter?"

"Yes he did, Holmes, but it was so desiccated and corrupt, that I thought it best not to bring it with me."

"It is of no matter," said Holmes, "for in the unlikelihood that I am mistaken, upon examination you would find, that the kidney was not human and was probably that of a pig, which is of similar size and function to that of a human and would be easily obtainable from any shop such as those in Butcher's Row in Whitechapel. In addition, if we consider that the murderer had some medical experience, such as your suspect, Klosowski, he would have been able to efficiently preserve the kidney."

"So," said Abberline, "that means..."

"That both the letter or letters and the kidney are red herrings," interrupted Holmes, "and that any further pursuit along these lines would be counterproductive."

"Well then, Holmes, how should we proceed from here?"

"Let me ask you: What is Sir Charles Warren's opinion of all of this apparent folderol?"

"Sir Charles's opinion? It is interesting that you should pose that question, Holmes. In apparent frustration, Sir Charles resigned his position as Commissioner of Police yesterday morning and returned to the army. Although this may leave us somewhat rudderless, perhaps the situation will afford us more latitude in our investigation."

"Not altogether unexpected," said Holmes. "Moving forward, tell me more about poor Mrs. Kelly."

"Mrs. Kelly was discovered earlier today by her landlord's assistant when he went round to collect overdue rent on her ground floor flat. When he received no answer to his knock, he pushed aside a makeshift curtain and was assaulted by the sight of what remained of Mrs. Kelly on her bed."

At this, Abberline paused and covered his mouth as if he were on the verge of becoming ill.

"Are you all right, Abberline?" I asked. "Would you care for some water? Whisky, perhaps?"

"No, thank you, Watson. Just let me compose myself for a moment. In all my years on the police force, I have never witnessed such a scene as greeted me this morning.

"Mrs. Kelly, the poor soul, lay in her blood-soaked bed with her legs apart. She had been split from top to bottom, her abdominal cavity emptied of her viscera which had been spread beneath her head. Her breasts had been removed, and her face virtually hacked away. I tell you, Holmes, the term 'madman' does not approach the creature that committed this atrocity! I think I would like that drink now, if you don't mind."

"Of course," said Holmes. "Watson, if you would."

I complied and sat back to listen and take notes.

Once Abberline had regained his balance, Holmes continued. "It appears that our Jack has either become more careful or he experienced no small amount of serendipity in that this latest act was perpetrated indoors. He was not running the risk of being discovered, so he could take his time, which he undoubtedly did. It did not matter if he was seen going into Miller's Court, since that would have been a normal occurrence of a doxy with her client. Once inside, as was his method of operation, Mrs. Kelly was strangled to stop her heart and to prevent any noise from escaping and causing alarm. Once this first step was accomplished, he could then proceed to apply his malignant ministrations to the poor woman at his leisure."

Abberline nodded thoughtfully and took a sip of his drink. "What is your recommendation, Holmes?"

"I certainly do not intend to discourage any efforts on the part of Scotland Yard, Abberline, but I fear that without some sort of dramatic breakthrough, such as a confession or the emergence of an actual eyewitness to the assaults, which is highly unlikely, London may have heard the last of Jack the Ripper, at least for a time."

"What do you mean, Holmes?"

"You must understand, Abberline, this is not a guess, for as I have said in the past, I never guess. Guessing is a shocking habit destructive to the logical faculty. Rather, this is a legitimate and logical conjecture on my part co-based on the empirical evidence present and information I have gleaned from the writings and observations of Krafft-Ebing. As I have mentioned previously, the nature of the assaults could very well be indicative of the acting out of an aberrant sexual urge. I believe that this latest atrocity may be evidence that this urge was brought to its ultimate fulfilment—completion as it were. His hypersexuality brought to consummation, at least temporarily. With the fiend's desires sated perhaps to the point of some satisfaction, logic and reason may well have taken control of his actions in that he has decided that at this point, as Shakespeare had it, "the better part of valour is discretion." He must be acutely aware of the growing efforts to apprehend him as the levels of alarm and panic likewise increase. Therefore, it is only logical to conclude that he would heed the danger surrounding him and choose to curtail his activities or perhaps even desert the area for more fertile fields. Immigration is not out of the question."

"What are we to do, then?"

"My advice to you," said Holmes as he rose to escort Abberline to the door, "is to continue your investigations in the manner in which you have been conducting them. One should never eliminate the possibilities of a revelation no matter how remote. Certainly you should maintain the surveillance of your prime suspects, particularly your Mr. Klosowski. My instincts tell me that you may be onto something there.

"But, my dear Abberline, I would not have high expectations at this point. And certainly, when no further murders crop up that could be laid at the feet of Jack the Ripper, Scotland Yard will necessarily revert to its primary duties and move on to more promising cases. In the meantime, please feel free to call on Watson and myself at any time. We remain at your service. Godspeed."

Part I

Chapter Five

Once Abberline had left us, I said, "Holmes, do you really think that we have heard the last of Jack the Ripper? Is there no hope for the apprehension of the fiend?"

"For the present, Watson, and only for the present. I do believe he will strike again. Where and when are the only questions. He is obviously a crafty individual and may change his methods once his blood lust overcomes him again. This has been known to happen in other cases. On the other hand, his singular sexual psychopathy may evolve, or devolve as the case may be, into an alternative form altogether, mutilations no longer being satisfactory. All of which does not portend a rapid solution. Apprehension will take place, Watson, of that there can be no doubt, but more important at this point than diligence and deductive skill, is that we practice the admirable yet at times frustrating strategy of tactical patience. Patience will be the prime factor if we are to nick Jack the Ripper."

With that statement, Holmes refilled his pipe from the Persian slipper, lit it and retrieved a copy of *The Star,* which Mrs. Hudson had deposited outside our door. He then crossed to his armchair, sat and as he opened the paper announced, "There is nothing more to be said or done presently on the matter, Watson, which currently suits me well, for as I have told you in the past: I am in fact the most incurably lazy devil that ever stood in shoe leather. So, if you will allow me, I shall now indulge in my relaxation method of studying and observing life's trifles as they appear in this fine example of sensational journalism."

As we waited for any further developments of police investigation into the Whitechapel horror, I took Holmes at his word and settled back into the sporadic reading of my volume of the medical student's adventures on an Arctic whaling ship.

For the remainder of the month of November and the better part of December, Holmes and I occupied ourselves with various minor consultations with both the police and private citizens, the complaints of whom hardly merit mention save for the fact that they each presented factors that sparked Holmes's interest and served as minor exercises for his deductive skills. They also served to divert him from his cocaine predilection. I have not chronicled them any further than this mention.

Shortly after Christmas, Abberline paid us a further visit in the wake of the discovery of yet another murder victim in Whitechapel, in Clarke's Yard in High Street. She had been strangled. At first Holmes was somewhat disappointed in that he was under the impression that Abberline had brought this killing to our attention as being another victim of the Ripper. Due to the nature of the crime and the complete lack of any attempt at mutilation, Holmes had already discounted this as a possibility when the murder was first reported in the newspapers earlier in the month. The victim had only recently been identified as a prostitute named Rose Mylett. To Holmes's relief, Abberline asserted that adhering to Holmes's analysis and recommendations, he had also discounted this latest murder as being completely unrelated to the Ripper murders. He only wanted to apprise Holmes that Scotland

Yard, under his authority as chief of the detective corps, was conducting the investigation based on Holmes's methodology.

Abberline did not linger and with Holmes's encouragement to persevere, took his leave.

The remainder of the year and the turn of 1889 brought us precious little in the way of new cases. I kept up with my practice on a more-or-less part-time basis, while Holmes and I worked on refining my notes on our adventures. In the meanwhile, as much time as I could devise, I spent in my continued courtship of Miss Mary Morstan, who exhibited no small degree of patience herself, considering the life into which she would marry.

April brought us the adventure of a Miss Violet Hunter, in whom Holmes, during the process of solving the mystery, appeared curiously enough to develop a more than cliental relationship. For a short time, this had me in hopes of the possibility of joint nuptials. As it resolved itself however, Holmes's interest in Miss Hunter, save for the ironic fact that she possessed the same Christian name as his mother, revolved purely around the nature of the mystery and faded with its solution.

On the first day of May, Miss Mary Morstan and I were married in St. Mark's Church in Camberwell, my first wife, Constance Adams, having succumbed to pneumonia in late 1887, with Mr. Sherlock Holmes serving as my best man, of course. Shortly after the event, and in the effort to normalise my life somewhat, I had the opportunity to purchase a struggling practice in Paddington and with my bride moved into adjoining quarters there. Although my relationship with

Holmes was altered due to my practice and relocation, I was still able to continue my duties on a moderated basis as Holmes assistant, confidant and chronicler. After all, Holmes had once confided in me that he would be lost without his Boswell, so I could hardly desert him entirely, nor did I wish to do so.

In addition to several adventures that we encountered in the ensuing months of 1889, there were two further murders in Whitechapel that came under the scrutiny of Scotland Yard. Abberline assured us they were not worth our involvement as he had, by way of applying Holmes' criteria to the cases, determined that they were not perpetrated by our Ripper.

Dogged detective that he was, however, Abberline's surveillance of the suspect Klosowski had not diminished. In October, Abberline announced to us that Klosowski had met and married a Polish girl named Lucy Baderski and was now the proprietor of a barber shop in High Street in Whitechapel. He further remarked that Klosowski's behaviour still bordered on unsociable and his new wife appeared to bear the evidence of some physical distress. Holmes and I agreed that Abberline should continue a regular surveillance of Klosowski and emphasised again that patience was of the utmost importance.

The year of 1890 brought us three adventures in which I was able to participate and chronicle since I had become quite adept at successfully splitting my time between my Paddington residence and practice and Baker Street. None of these cases, although both unique and curious, had anything to do with the Whitechapel murders and as a consequence, we heard little of note from Abberline in the way of police business. Indeed there were no incidents to be connected with the Ripper in all of 1890.

It wasn't until February of 1891 that the newspapers announced another murder in Whitechapel. A prostitute named Frances Coles had been discovered by a constable shortly after she had been attacked, judging by the warmth of her body and the fact that the constable said that as he arrived on the scene, he heard retreating footsteps. Apparently, her attacker had been interrupted in his dastardly work, since though her throat had been viciously slashed, there were no further mutilations. According to Abberline, these details suggested that the Ripper had made another appearance. I am quite certain that Holmes would have been in agreement if he were present, but at that time, he was engaged on a commission from the French Government.

Putting into use Holmes's methods of deduction, I reached the following conclusion and related it to Abberline. Because this was the second occurrence of the Ripper nearly being apprehended while in the act and judging that the man, while deranged, was not foolish, I would not be surprised if there were to be an interval, not a cessation, to these atrocities. Discouraged, but no less steadfast in his determination to follow his instincts and the evidence, Abberline vowed to double his surveillance of Klosowski.

It came as no surprise then, when in early April, Holmes being still on the Continent, Abberline came to me with the news that Klosowski and his wife had emigrated to America, where he had opened a barber shop in the Lower East Side of Manhattan in New York City. I took some vicarious pleasure in the fact that the possibility of this occurrence had been advanced by Holmes as a likely tactic by the Whitechapel perpetrator. Speaking for my friend, I advised that Abberline persevere, which advice was unnecessary, as he concurred with our opinion that the case was far from concluded with Klosowski's move across the Atlantic.

As I have related in the adventure that I falsely titled *The Final Problem,* Holmes unexpectedly returned from France on the 24th of April, obsessed with the pursuit of Professor James Moriarty. He vigorously enjoined me to accompany him back to the Continent to assist in his mission. Though I was able to enlighten him as to Abberline's discoveries and Klosowski's disposition, he seemed to take the information in stride, stating that he had more pressing matters at the moment. He assured me he would devote his full attention to the Ripper affair when we returned from the Continent. He expressed supreme confidence that straightaway, we would together end the career of the nefarious Moriarty. In point of fact, the professor's depredations were indeed brought to a swift denouement on the 4th of May at the foot of the Reichenbach Falls in Switzerland. But oh the horrible bargain that was struck in the service of justice – or so I believed. For a time, nearly three years to be exact, I was certain that the Reichenbach Falls had also brought an end to my dear friend Mr. Sherlock Holmes. Locked as he was in Moriarty's death grip, he accompanied his nemesis over the falls to his death. I was devastated that the best and wisest man I had ever known was lost to me and to the world. To say that it created an unfillable void in my life is understating the fact.

Part I

Chapter Six

It was Holmes's brother, Mycroft, who insisted that the lodgings at 221B Baker Street not be disturbed. When he considered all the events and the possibilities of the goings on at the Reichenbach Falls, he refused to accept the reality of Holmes's demise. There were simply too many possible contingencies, too many unknown factors, and no *corpus delicti* for him to declare that his younger brother was in fact lost.

It was at Mycroft's suggestion and with the acquiescence of my dear wife, Mary, that I shortly thereafter sold my successful practice in Paddington and purchased a lesser one, with accompanying lodgings, in my former environs of Kensington. Thus I was afforded the opportunity to practice medicine on a part-time basis and devote my energies, as I now so fervently desired, to editing and revising my journals of the adventures of the world's first consulting detective.

To my eternal dismay, the year of 1891 brought yet another heartrending agony to my doorstep when my dear Mary contracted influenza. Despite the use of all my training and skills and ministering to her, utilising the most modern methods, she succumbed to the damnable disease in August. At that point, my life seemed to me to be of no further use. Somehow, I persevered, existing on the warmth of memories of days past.

The rest of the year progressed slower than I thought possible, disabled as I was by the perceived passing of the two people I treasured most. Having no family or kin with whom to commiserate and share my sadness, I was fortunate indeed that Mycroft insisted that I soldier on in my work, particularly in regard to my endeavours chronicling his brother's career. And so, I dutifully pressed on as the year passed.

In January of 1892, Abberline called on me to let me know that Klosowski's pregnant wife, Lucy, had returned to England and was now living with her sister, Alice, in Whitechapel. Klosowski, as far as could be determined, had remained in Jersey City, New Jersey, to where he had relocated from the Lower East Side of Manhattan.

Abberline also informed me that he was bringing to a close his nearly 30-year career with Scotland Yard and had decided to accept a position offered to him by William Pinkerton of the Pinkerton Detective Agency, which was seeking to extend its investigative branch outside of the continental United States. Abberline assured me that this employment would allow him a greater range of inquiry and freedom of movement in his pursuit of Jack the Ripper.

With Klosowski's relocation to the United States, Abberline had established and maintained a cooperative relationship with American authorities, especially with New York City Detective Bureau Chief Thomas Byrnes, regarding Klosowski's movements and activities. Byrnes had been following the Whitechapel murder investigations since the very beginning. He and Abberline were thus well-acquainted.

Abberline related to me that Inspector Byrnes had advised him that the previous April, the body of an aging prostitute named Carrie Brown had been discovered in her lodgings in a run-down boarding house in an area of the city much like Whitechapel. She had been manually strangled and then viciously mutilated. Byrnes noted the similarities to the murder of Mary Jane Kelly and had only recently communicated as much to Abberline. Although Byrnes strongly suspected that the murders could have been committed by the Ripper, he had been circumspect with the information in order to avoid widespread panic, such as had occurred in London.

Over the following six months, three more murders were committed in the general area of New York City, all of which matched the Ripper's modus operandi, as reported by Chief Inspector Byrnes to Abberline, who passed the information on to me. In the middle of July, Abberline bitterly announced that Scotland Yard had officially closed the Ripper investigation. This was particularly galling to him as it had been reported that Klosowski had arrived back in England just the month before and had tried to resume cohabitation with his wife, who had given birth to a baby girl in May. Klosowski abruptly left, apparently at the insistence of Lucy, her sister; and her sister's husband, Stanislaus.

How I wished more than ever that Holmes were with me at this point, for I was still grieving over my poor Mary and could barely concentrate on my practice or Holmes's adventures. I fear I was of no assistance to Abberline, other than dutifully keeping a record of what he reported.

However, this information stimulated lessons which I had been fortunate enough to have absorbed from Holmes. Reasoning that as an alternative, however insufficient to Holmes being on the scene, I would try to put into practice his methodology. One of Holmes's prime tenets is that there is nothing more deceptive than an obvious fact. Further, it is his contention that the world is indeed full of obvious things which no one by any chance ever observes. What these precepts seemed to cry out for, as Holmes himself had put it, was "Data! Data! Data!"

Acting upon this, I requested that Abberline, by way of his still friendly connections with Scotland Yard, try to arrange an interview with the wronged, troubled, and perhaps endangered, Lucy Klosowski as soon as possible. I offered the opinion that it would be only fitting that the interview take place at 221B Baker Street, to which I still possessed a key. The atmosphere there would lend legitimacy to our inquiry without any discomfiture that might arise in the offices of the Pinkerton Detective Agency or Scotland Yard for that matter. Abberline was in full concurrence. I alerted Mycroft and Mrs. Hudson to our plans and a meeting was arranged for two days hence.

Part I
Chapter Seven

It was a pleasant mid-summer's day when Abberline and Lucy arrived at the door of 221B Baker Street. Apprised of our guest and the nature of the visitation, Mrs. Hudson had been kind enough to prepare tea in order to establish a friendly and welcoming atmosphere. I asked her to remain while the introductions were made and to put the young woman at ease. I opened the door and in stepped Abberline with a young lady on his arm.

Employing Holmesian powers of observation, I noted that though she was probably in her early 20s, her complexion, facial wear and her carriage indicated that her life had not been without care. Testifying to her Polish ancestry, were her blond hair, high cheekbones and blue eyes, which though rheumy were alert, a state which could very well evince emotional strain and or trepidation. She was of average height but slightly stooped, conceivably from the lingering effect of a physical malady, she had after all recently given birth. Owing to her reason for being here and her readiness to comply with the invitation, I thought that perhaps the cause of her slouch was of a more malicious nature. Her simple dress and hat were somewhat on the worn side and while hardly stylish, were entirely respectable. Mrs. Hudson took her hand.

"Hello, my dear, you are very welcome. I'm Mrs. Hudson, I take care of Dr. Watson and Mr. Holmes, when he is here. I am so glad Inspector Abberline brought you today. I am certain they can be of great help to you. I've set out a tea service for you. Help you relax. I'll leave you to your conversation now. If you need anything at all, don't hesitate to ask Dr. Watson. I'll be just downstairs and he'll ring me."

"Thank you Mrs. Hudson," I said as I held the door for her. "Now then, Lucy, if I may call you Lucy, as you've probably surmised, I'm Dr. John Watson. You may have heard of me from my association with Mr. Sherlock Holmes."

"Oh yes sir, I have heard of you. Will Mr. Holmes be joining us?" she asked with obvious hopefulness.

I confess I had not anticipated that question. "No, I'm afraid not, Lucy." Not wishing to cause her alarm or to dissuade her from talking with us, I continued, "Mr. Holmes is following another case on the Continent. I can assure you however, that when you speak with us, you are speaking with him. Isn't that right, Abberline?"

"Indeed it is, Watson. You are in the best of hands, Lucy."

"Thank you both," she said. "To be truthful with you I am nearly out of my mind with fear for my life and my little Cecilia. At the moment she is with my sister and her husband at their home in Scarborough Street"

"I see," I said. "Well we are here to help. In order to do that, we will need to know everything about your situation. Is that agreeable to you?"

"Oh yes."

"Please, make yourself comfortable on the sofa. There. Now, may I pour you a cup of tea?"

"Yes, please, with just milk, thank you"

Abberline and I decided to forgo the tea as we sat in chairs pulled up opposite the sofa. "Now then, you are married to Severin Klosowski, correct?"

"Yes it is, Doctor, only now how I wish it were not so."

"Ah then, that alone tells us much," I said as I looked at Abberline.

"Perhaps," said Abberline, "you might start at the beginning, from when you met."

"As you know, we are both of Polish roots, though I have been here longer. We met at a function at the Polish Club in Clerkenwell in October of 1889. I was attracted to him immediately. He was quite striking, solid, with his dark hair and moustache and eyes that seemed to go right into me, didn't they. He was very intelligent and very sure of himself, commanding I might say. That should have warned me, but foolish me I was swept away and scarcely five weeks later we were married."

"I take it all went well at first?"

"At first, yeah it did. He had a job as a barber and he was good at it, don't you know. He had his own shop for a while and when business slowed down, he had no problem finding work at other shops."

"So he was a good provider then, a good husband?" I asked.

"Oh I suppose, but from the start, he didn't like staying home nights. Some nights he'd go out and not come back until three or four in the morning. When I'd question him about it, he'd get awfully angry with me about a wife's role being to obey her husband and all. After I got pregnant, he was out almost every night and sometimes came home stinking and top-heavy from the drink. That was when his temper got the best of him and he'd take it out on me."

"Physically?"

"Sometimes," she hesitated then quickly added, "but I blame myself for questioning him too much, you know, what with the strain he was under at work and all. And he seemed to be angry with the baby coming; that was only more strain on him, wasn't it?"

Abberline turned to me, "Don't be shocked, Watson. In my experiences with the Yard, I've found that many abused wives have felt that way. It is only another case of mistreatment wrought by their husbands. It is a mental abuse that goes hand in glove with the physical abuse and is perhaps more damaging and longer lasting."

"I see." I turned to Lucy. "It's not your fault, Lucy, not at all. You are the victim in all of this.

"Oh I know that now right enough, Dr. Watson. I know that now!"

"I am very glad to hear it, my dear. Now please continue."

"Yes sir. I gave birth to a little boy in January of 1891."

"How did that affect your marriage?"

"Well, to begin with, the poor thing was not quite healthy from the very start. That only made things at home more difficult, don't you know. Severin was not happy. He was staying out late longer and sometimes not coming home at all. It was like he was angry almost all the time. Of course, when he was sober, he told me he loved me and all, but that would change when he'd come home drunk.

"I can see how that must have taken a toll on you."

"Indeed it did. I got sick myself, didn't I. Fever and chills and all. My little Walter, that's what we'd named the baby, he kept fighting away and seemed to be doing better, but he kept coughing and was hot to the touch. Suddenly in March, it was like the poor little thing just gave up and died, at least that was how Severin broke the news to me, me being bundled up in my sister's room."

"Excuse me," said Abberline, "Severin was with your baby when he died?"

"Why, yes, he was."

"Was there anyone else with him?"

"No, my sister was with me and her husband was at work. Severin took it upon himself to contact the doctor. Of course he had had considerable medical training, so he did all he could and then went for the doctor, but it was all over by then. Little Walter was gone and then he came to tell me."

At that, Lucy began to sob. I offered her my handkerchief and my hand upon her shoulder as I turned to Abberline. I could tell by his expression that he was of the same mind as I; circumstantial evidence can be very compelling. In just a minute or thereabout, Lucy seemed to recover. "Do you feel up to continuing?"

"Oh yes," she said. "I'm so sorry."

"It's all right, we understand," said Abberline, "Please, take your time and continue when you wish."

"Yes, thank you. I'm fine now. It all happened so quickly after that; Severin decided that we should try for a fresh start in America. It would be what we both needed: A new life in the new world, as they put it. And so with what little we had, after making arrangements for little Walter to be put to rest with my brother-in-law's family, I bade goodbye to my sister and her husband, and on April 1st, we set sail for America and the altogether grand city of New York.

"To make short of it, where we were in New York, it was the same as Whitechapel; there were no streets paved with gold. A new life in a new world...Hah! Severin found a job all right, but he hadn't changed a whit. He was still out until all hours of the night until late in the month when all of a sudden he announced we were moving to New Jersey. It was only about five miles from where we were living but it was a whole nother state, wasn't it!"

"When was this, do you recall?"

"Let's see, it was late in the summer, as I said. I think it was on the 25th of August. Severin was able to open a barber shop in Jersey City. We lived in rooms behind the shop. To be honest, Severin was a good provider and in the early part of our time in New Jersey, I thought we really would start a new life, didn't I, and not long after, I was again with child.

"Almost at the same time, Severin picked up his old ways again: He was out until all hours, and coming home angry and drunk, he'd sometimes beat me about. It was all I could do to stay with him for the sake of the child inside me."

She started to weep again. "You poor woman," I said, "I should think you had endured enough at that point."

"You'd think so, wouldn't you, "she said as she wiped her tears, "but no. But it weren't long in coming. This was in the afternoon early this January. We were having one of our usual quarrels in our rooms at the barber shop. This one was special, though. He got me down on the bed with my arms underneath me. He pressed his face against my mouth and nose so I couldn't scream. I couldn't even breathe. He had his hands round my throat! I was nearly out when all of a sudden he stopped. A customer had come into the shop and called for him. And business was always business with Severin, don't you know, so he got up off me and went into the shop."

"For the love of God, woman, what did you do?"

"Well, I started to come to my senses and tried to get up from the floor, where he had tossed me when he rose. I looked at the bed and saw a wooden handle poking out from under the pillow. I pulled it out and saw that it was a knife, a very sharp knife"

"My word, Lucy! Surely you must have fled at that point?" said Abberline.

"Don't I know it?" she said. "But, and you can call me silly, for some reason I had to know his intentions."

"His intentions!" Abberline and I both screamed in unison.

"I know," she said, "I know. I composed myself, hid the knife in my satchel, put on my hat and coat, sat on the bed and waited until his customer had left. Severin came back into the room much calmed and at ease. I stood. He looked at the pillow where the knife had been hidden, looked at me, smiled and gave a short laugh.

"'And just how far were you going to go this time, Severin?' I asked him. He laughed and turned away. I crossed to the door. 'Ah, my dear Lucy,' he said, 'the time has come for us to part hasn't it? My plan, if only that customer hadn't interrupted me, was to cut your pretty little head off – after you were dead, of course, I didn't want you to suffer through that mess, and then to put you to rest under the floorboards in that far corner.' I kept backing toward the door. Severin stared at me and lit a cigarette. 'But what of the neighbours?' I asked. 'The neighbours would have asked where I had gone to.' He exhaled smoke and shrugged his shoulders, 'Oh, I should simply have told them that you had gone back to New York.' Then he laughed. That was my chance. I ran out the door and took refuge with a neighbour.

"We kept watch on the shop until nighttime, and Severin left on one of his rambles. With the help of friends, I then went back to the shop, collected what few things that were mine and the readies we had stashed away, which I also figured I was entitled to, don't you?"

"Indeed we do, Lucy, at the very least. And then?"

"And then," she sighed, "again with the help of friends, I was able to make arrangements and secured passage here, thank God."

"Thank God indeed, Lucy," I said. "Did he try to find you?"

"No, he didn't, so far as I know."

Abberline interjected, "I would be most surprised if he had tried. He undoubtedly wanted Lucy out of his life and was

54

certain he had frightened her right out of the country and indeed out of his life. Did you think of going to the authorities?"

"I did at first, but who would take the word of a poor little confused immigrant girl against that of her husband, who was a respected member of the business community?"

"She may have a point there, Abberline," I said.

"Quite," said Abberline. "In addition, if our suspicions are correct, he did search for her because he did not want to bring any undue attention to himself that might connect him in any way to the Ripper-like murders that had taken place while he had been residing in America."

"I had wondered about that, myself," Lucy said. "In truth though, I was so glad to be away from there, away from him and back here in England with my dear sister and her husband, Stanislas, again. The house in Scarborough Street was a safe place and when little Cecelia came along in May, we were all happy for a while."

"He came back though, didn't he?" I asked.

"Oh he did, indeed, Doctor, but not for long. I don't know how he found out about the baby, but I suppose he wanted to see her for himself. He got as far as the door. All his sweet talk and apologising and smarmy charm didn't hold water with me and especially not with Stanislas. You see, wasn't it Stanislas who first introduced us at the Polish Club, and he was feeling awfully guilty ever since. He explained to Severin very clear like, that it might not be too healthy for him if he were to ever come near any of us ever again. And he was going to make sure that Scotland Yard knew that he was back in England and what had happened to me in America. That did it for Severin. The penny dropped and with a smile that chilled me to my bones, he nodded, backed away, turned and disappeared into Whitechapel."

"Do you have any idea where he might have gone?" I asked.

"No sir, but if I was to guess, I'd say he was off to a pub looking for a drink and some doxy he could charm. If you don't mind now, Doctor, I'd like to be getting back to my Cecelia. All of this has brought back bad memories, don't you know. I really don't have anything else to tell you about Severin other than he is dangerous. You should keep a close watch on him, you should."

"You can rest assured of that Lucy," said Abberline. "I am working with the Pinkerton detectives now and together with some friends from Scotland Yard, your Mr. Severin Klosowski will be under careful surveillance. You have nothing to fear."

"Thank you, Inspector, but I had so hoped Mr. Holmes would be involved, didn't I."

"Not to worry, my dear," I hastened to add. "Mr. Holmes will be involved as much as is humanly possible." I did not feel that I was telling an untruth and that by offering that somewhat cloudy placation, I helped to allay her anxiety. Nonetheless, Abberline rolled his eyes.

"Thank you, Doctor, I am much relieved," she said as she heaved a sigh.

"Now," I continued as I took her hand, "I know that Inspector Abberline will be glad to accompany you back to Scarborough Street. You have been most gracious and helpful.

I know that I speak for Mr. Holmes when I say that we both wish the best for you and your new baby girl. Please feel free to call on us in the future if there is any way we might be of assistance. Abberline, if you will?"

After seeing Lucy home, Abberline returned to Baker Street and we conferred on the information the poor girl had provided. We agreed that Klosowski was indeed a foul individual and our suspicions were only encouraged by his behaviour here and in America toward women and especially by the declaration to Lucy of his murderous intent. He was still the most likely candidate to be the Ripper. Even with this, Abberline was absolutely correct when he said that we should muster our forces to keep a heavy observation on Klosowski. Barring some change in circumstances or solid revelations, that was all we could do for the foreseeable future.

Klosowski had been relatively safe from British authorities while he was in America, though he could not know that Abberline, by way of Chief Inspector Byrnes, was being kept apprised of his activities. Perhaps he felt that investigations into the Ripper-like murders in America were coming too close to him and that enough time had passed that London could provide him with some degree of security, at least until his passions once again took control of him. By returning to London, he was, in fact, returning to the scene of his greatest successes.

Part II
Chapter One

For the rest of 1892, I heard from Abberline roughly every four to six weeks. He had nothing substantive to report on any of Klosowski's comings and goings. Klosowski had secured a position as an assistant in a hair salon in Tottenham and appeared to be leading an unexceptional life. Of course his evening wanderings continued without abatement, as noted by surveilling operatives and Abberline himself. Fortunately, Klosowski made no further attempts to contact Lucy. At loose ends, I found myself leaning on the advice Holmes had given me during our adventure at Baskerville Hall, which was to have patience, which was put to the test over the ensuing months. How I so missed Holmes: the melancholy only increased as I laboured on the accounts of our adventures.

I would occasionally call in at the Diogenes club to confer with Mycroft and to have him reassure me of his optimism about the survival of his brother. I otherwise had my practice on which to concentrate which, I must confess, at this point only served as a diversion for me. Of course I was cautious, careful and professional as ever in the performance of my medical duties but still, this was now only a side-line and a mere occupation rather than a calling, such as it deserved to be treated.

One day in November of 1893, I had just returned from an encouraging and palliative visit with Mycroft Holmes when Abberline called on me at my office in Kensington. He bore intriguing and rather strange news in regard to Mr. Klosowski.

It seems that in the course of his latest employment as a hairdresser, he had struck up an acquaintance with a woman. This acquaintance had matured and flowered to the point wherein they set up lodging together. Even though Klosowski was still legally married to Lucy at the time, that was not the most outlandish aspect of the relationship. The woman's name was Annie Georgina Chapman. According to Abberline, she was the daughter of the Ripper's third Whitechapel victim, Annie Chapman. Just what this bizarre turn of events indicated, I could not tell. If ever there were a time when Holmes's powers of reasoning were called for, this was certainly it.

Throughout the winter and into the spring of 1894, Klosowski and Annie were in a common law, yet bigamous, marriage. He continued with his chosen occupation, but as witnessed by neighbours and surveillance officers, he also kept up his nightly wanderings and the unseemly, harsh, though not quite illegal treatment of his so-called new wife.

All the while, Abberline and I could do nothing except keep watch on Klosowski, waiting for him to make a mistake or somehow to reveal his intentions. I was in a state of simmering frustration, stewing on the conundrum at hand when on evening of the 5th of April I took a head-clearing stroll through Hyde Park. Of course you will understand why that date is seared into my memory, for that was when my prayers were answered and my friend and colleague Mr. Sherlock Holmes returned from the dead and revealed himself to me.

As anxious as I was to enlighten Holmes on the matter of Mr. Severin Klosowski, Holmes prevailed upon me to help him bring an end to his efforts of the past three years which were, as he explained to me, the apprehension of the second most dangerous man in London, Colonel Sebastian Moran. Moran, as you know, had been the only witness to the death of Professor Moriarty at the Reichenbach Falls and the survival of Holmes by way of his mastery of baritsu. Holmes had spent the last three years in travel, study and even some government work. It also included efforts to outwit Moran who was filled with grim determination to put an end to Mr. Sherlock Holmes and avenge Moriarty's death. He apologised for keeping me in the dark, for my own protection actually, further noting that he had maintained contact with Mycroft over the three years so that he might have access to operational funds. He asked for my assistance and that of Mrs. Hudson that evening so that he might bring his quest as well as the nefarious activities of Colonel Moran to a close. It all transpired as I reported it in *The Adventure of the Empty House,* culminating with Moran being taken into custody by our old Scotland Yard associate, Inspector Lestrade.

Following a joyous and informative evening and dinner spent with Holmes, during which he enlightened me on a number of the particulars of his activities and travels over the past three years, we both retired to our rooms at 221B Baker Street. The next morning, brimming with energy and inquisitiveness, Holmes fairly assaulted me with questions regarding Abberline's efforts in the Ripper investigation.

"Of course," he said, "I have followed along as much as was possible in the newspapers, but recently there seems to be a dearth of information on the case, almost as if Scotland Yard has given up the ghost."

"I am afraid that is it exactly, Holmes," I said. I went on to tell him of Scotland Yard's official abandonment of the case, Abberline's retirement two years ago, his following enlistment with the Pinkerton Detective Agency, and how he now was essentially conducting a one-man inquiry.

"I understand, Watson. We must remedy the situation, if at all possible," he said as he crossed to the mantel and examined the Persian slipper of three-year-old tobacco.

I looked after him and after a moment asked, "We?"

"Certainly, my dear fellow. You do not for one instant think that I could function with any degree of certitude in these now more perilous times without you? My continued success as a consulting detective and therefore the achievement of justice in a dangerous world can only exist with the able assistance of my stalwart companion. You are more than my Boswell. You are my dear friend and partner."

I was struck dumb. I knew our bond was unique, but Holmes has never taken pains to verbalise it as such.

"Are you amenable?" he asked.

"Of course I am, Holmes! I've not been waiting these three years for nothing. Of course I am amenable."

"Splendid," he said.

Suddenly, the smile faded from Holmes' face. "Forgive me old fellow. I have visited my negligence upon you in more ways than one. Out of necessity, I kept you in the dark these past years and for that, I am sincerely sorry. I never intended you any pain. Secondly, I read in the journals about the passing of your dear Mary. Of course you have my deepest sympathy, my friend."

Uncomfortable as he was at open displays of emotion, Holmes abruptly turned to the business at hand. "Now then, since we appear to have our work cut out for us, I think it would be most advantageous if you were to sell or lease your practice in Kensington and relocate here with me at our old lodgings in Baker Street."

Nothing could have pleased me more. In fact earlier in the week I had been approached by a young doctor named Horace Verner, who had inquired about the possibility of purchasing my practice. As it turned out, Dr. Verner was a cousin of Holmes who had, of course, put the entire transaction in motion, knowing that I would readily agree. So it was that in the spring of 1894 the game, which had begun six years earlier, was once again afoot.

Part II
Chapter Two

I began by apprising Holmes of the fact that Klosowski and his wife, Lucy, had left England for America shortly after a final Ripper-attributed murder in early 1891, during which he had nearly been caught. Holmes had replied that this was not surprising and that he had indeed predicted such a move from the suspect.

I further informed him of the four murders bearing Ripper-like characteristics that had been perpetrated in the vicinity of Klosowski's residences in New York and New Jersey over the course of slightly more than a year. Holmes found this somewhat interesting but hardly more than circumstantial and therefore, in this instance, of only indicative and not superlative importance.

I then told him of Lucy's testimony to Abberline and myself, describing her assault and attempted murder at the hands of her husband, the admission of his lethal plans, her subsequent escape back to England and birth of her daughter. All of these events were capped with the unwelcome return of Klosowski to England and his supposed attempt at reconciliation.

The information about Klosowski's attack on Lucy in January of 1892 brought about a most surprising reaction from Holmes; he smiled. Turning to me, he said, "Watson, I believe that we have been correct all along. We should be grateful to Abberline for having brought Klosowski to our attention in the first place. His instincts were precisely correct right from the beginning. Taken as a whole, Klosowski's actions are testimony that he is a man of devious intelligence."

"But Holmes," I said, "the man is insane!"

"Oh he is clearly insane, Watson, but that takes nothing away from his intelligence, which he has been able to apply to his insane and thoroughly evil tendencies. Mark you, he is no Moriarty or even Moran, but his depredations may be perceived to be all the more heinous for the grisly nature of the attacks on individual and unsuspecting females.

"He is a crafty one, Watson. See how he fled to America after he was nearly apprehended in England. Then considering the particulars of the murders that took place in America and the ensuing investigations, he perhaps sensed that he was coming under suspicion there and so returned to England at a time when an interest in the original Whitechapel murders had subsided. Because of this, he assumed that he would be safe on home soil to perhaps continue his unholy practices.

"I am also quite certain that he fully intended to kill Lucy because he was tired of her and also did not want the burden of a new baby. He was just as happy to frighten her out of the country as a temporary solution while he assessed his position in order to decide his next move. The fact that he sought her out after returning to England is evidence of the twisted machinations of his mind and was most certainly a demented play for some kind of control."

"Holmes, you know that I am loath to interrupt while you are in the deductive process, but I feel that I must do so at this point."

"Very well, Watson. I am certain you have good reason. What is it?"

"The strangest turn of this entire concern is what I am about to reveal to you now. Last autumn, Klosowski took up with another woman and began living with her."

"Yes?"

"The woman was Annie Georgina Chapman, the daughter of one of the Ripper's early victims."

"Ah ha!" said Holmes. "You see what has happened here? By taking up with this woman, he is *de facto* returning to the scene of the crime. That she is the daughter of one of his victims is a declaration of his omnipotence and control. It also indicates that he looks at his entire style of living as a lark, a game if you will, one in which he has the upper hand and is flaunting it in the face of the authorities though they are unaware of it. Judging by the nature of the man, I would say that once he learned the identity of this new woman, he couldn't resist taking her as a conquest."

"Wait," I said, "it gets even all the more strange. In a short time, Annie became with child and at this point, Klosowski brought another woman home to join their household. You'll never guess the name of that woman."

"Watson, I do believe that the woman was none other than Lucy Klosowski."

"Holmes, this is too much. Surely you did not hazard a guess?"

"As you are aware, Watson, I never guess, the practice is destructive to the logical faculty. I'm shocked that you would suggest it."

"Then how?…"

"Klosowski's behaviour, as I remarked when the Ripper murders were first brought to our attention, is partially the blame of an abnormal sexual motivation. It was also spurred on by an unnatural and overwhelming sense of superiority and quest for power and control. He was not at all satisfied to let go of Lucy while she, though she claimed to be well rid of him, still retained an attraction for the man and he saw that. She could not dismiss the fact that Klosowski was the father of her children and though he was beastly toward her, she had remained by his side since 1889. Judging by her behaviour, she was in fact trapped in a self-abusive situation, being entirely incapable of breaking out once he contacted her again. I should note, Watson, that this illogical and demeaning behaviour on Lucy's part is not all that uncommon among women who have been repeatedly beaten by their husbands.. It is certainly not their fault, yet they somehow blame themselves for the harsh treatment they receive at the hands of their husbands."

"Quite right, Holmes. In fact, Lucy mentioned feelings of guilt during our interrogative session. My word, Holmes, how I have missed you! I'm grateful that your deductive and analytical powers have not diminished in the slightest during your three-year hiatus."

I was about to quiz Holmes for any further thoughts when Mrs. Hudson's rap at the door and subsequent entry brought Inspector Abberline into the room. "Watson, I must share with you the most recent...Holmes! You've returned from the dead!"

"Really Abberline, I am flattered that you have such confidence in my uncanny abilities, but I can assure you of only two things: I was never dead and I have returned. Furthermore, I am delighted to see you again. Watson has brought me up to date with your machinations in the Ripper matter. I must say, I am much impressed with your diligence. As you are doubtless aware, the more outre and grotesque the incident or, in this case series of incidents, the more carefully it deserves to be examined. My compliments."

"Thank you, Holmes. And I do want to hear of your adventures and how you've come back to us, but now I have news that I believe you'll find quite interesting."

I could not resist, "Out with it then, Abberline, by all means."

He turned toward Holmes. "Has Watson informed you of the recent development regarding Klosowski taking up residence with both his legal wife, Lucy, and his common law wife, Annie?

"He has."

"Well, sir, I am here to announce that that singular connubial relationship is at an end. Annie and Lucy have both taken their leave from the abode of Mr. Severin Klosowski."

"Brava to them!" I said.

"Brava, indeed," said Holmes. "I am quite certain that the move has saved both of their lives."

"But there's more!" said Abberline. "It appears that not only is there no longer any state of conjugal bliss in the Klosowski abode, there is no longer a Klosowski."

"Abberline!" I cried, "you can't possibly mean that Klosowski is dead?"

"There now, Watson," said Holmes in a calming manner. "I am quite certain that is not what the good inspector meant. Is that not so, Abberline?"

"You are correct, Holmes. Our man Klosowski has taken leave of his lodgings and despite being surveilled, seems to have disappeared into the bowels of Whitechapel. By way of conscientious investigation and legwork, a man answering to Klosowski's description was found to be employed at a barbershop in Leytonstone. I surreptitiously visited the site in person and confirmed that this was indeed our man. By way of discreet inquiry, I discovered that this individual was now calling himself George Chapman."

"Excellent!" exclaimed Holmes. "This is a display of the man's cunning and his weakness. I could not be more convinced than ever that this is the Ripper."

"What do you mean, Holmes? I don't quite understand," I said.

"I am certain Abberline will concur that one of the most reasonable methods employed by malefactors to avoid apprehension is to relocate from the area where they are known to be. In this case, Klosowski, or Chapman as we will now call him, removed himself a fair distance from Whitechapel, yet remained in East London, undoubtedly because he felt relatively comfortable in similar environs. In addition, taking an alias or in his case an apparently new identity altogether, would further stymie any pursuit."

"Yes, I see now how that works to his advantage, but how did that betray a weakness?"

"It's the new name itself: George Chapman. It is not uncommon wherein a felon may want to retain a souvenir, reminder or prize, if you will, of his crime as some sort of warped trophy. You might liken this to the way the Ripper absconded with some organs of a number of earlier victims. In this case, Chapman took his new Christian name from the middle name of his latest companion: Annie Georgina Chapman. His new surname, Chapman, of course is a souvenir in itself and an expression of power and superiority. He took her mother's life as well as the surname of the woman and her child.

"This is not only a case of re-visiting the crime, but of owning it and broadcasting it, flung in the collective faces of all those who would bring him to justice here and in America. Klosowski has disappeared. He no longer exists and yet here he is hiding in plain sight."

"That is all fascinating, Holmes, but where does it leave us? What is our course of action now?

"Ah now, Watson. I fear that our actions, such as they are, will be constrained, alas, to the dutiful exercise of that indispensable tool of investigation: patience. As you are aware, though long-term patience is not my strong suit, I am willing to apply it forcefully until justice is served. So we are in the position of being kept apprised by Abberline of his efforts by way of surveillance with the possible assistance of the Pinkertons and perhaps Scotland Yard. Are you willing, Abberline?"

"More than ever, Holmes, more than ever. I realised that we had uncovered some valuable information, but was uncertain as to how to apply it to our quest. From your explanations, I have come to realise the extent of Klosowski's – excuse me – Chapman's intelligence, craftiness and sense of self-preservation, even though he labours through the curse of criminal insanity."

"I believe we will find," said Holmes, "as time goes by, his methods may alter, perhaps by design or by a deviation in the urges that are harboured in his diseased and dangerous mind. It is my opinion then, from what I can deduce from Chapman's attitudes, behaviour and habits, our patience will be sorely tested as we proceed to obtain justice and solve this most complicated of cases, but solve it we must and solve it we ultimately will."

Part II

Chapter Three

The rest of the year 1894 brought us no new information regarding Mr. George Chapman. Abberline and his operatives kept watch on the man, but the only thing that stood out in his behaviour was that he was not cohabitating with a woman. By now claiming to be an American barber from New Jersey, he conducted his business in a responsible manner during the day. His nightly sojourns amongst the lower strata of society in search of female companionship never ebbed. In addition, by all accounts, his conduct toward these women had not mellowed, though it did not approach the severity of which we knew him capable.

Holmes and I concluded a very busy year indeed, which yielded a letter of thanks for our efforts in a particular matter from the President of France and the presentation of that country's Legion of Honour. We also experienced an adventure that took us to Chatham in Kent and the unfortunate business of the suicide of Professor Coram's expatriate Russian wife.

April of 1895, brought us news from Abberline that Chapman had found a new companion in the person of one Mary Spink, the alcoholic wife of a railway porter. In looking into the background of Mrs. Spink, Abberline found that she had come from some money which fact, together with her social habits, found her to be attractive to and compatible with our Mr. Chapman.

The year passed with Holmes and myself entangled in a number of interesting cases until Abberline brought us news

71

in October that Mary Spink had become the new Mrs. Chapman, though both were still married to other people. The agreement was a fortuitous one for Chapman, for Mary's grandfather had passed on and left her with a legacy of roughly £600. According to Abberline, Chapman took advantage of Mary's inheritance and with it, re-located and opened a barbershop in Hastings.

We had a dearth of cases in 1896, until late in the year, which lengthy inactivity in the past gave me cause to worry about my good friend. As you are aware, Holmes was always interested in the latest advances in the study of medicine and the human mind as they might be applied to his work as a detective. Consequently he had become quite taken by the work of Dr. Sigmund Freud, among which was his advocacy of the use of cocaine. He claimed, along with Freud, that use of the drug was transcendentally stimulating and clarifying to the mind. In the past, Holmes had acted upon this belief and against my advice had often turned to the drug during periods of inaction.

However, Dr. Freud had come to the realisation that cocaine was in fact inhibiting and limiting his intellectual performance and repudiated his former advocacy of the drug. Following Holmes's return from the dead, so to speak, he made it a point to alert me to the fact that he now decried the use of the drug in any form. I can only assume that he must have experienced an epiphany regarding the stimulant sometime during his three-year hiatus. At any rate, by now, his cocaine use was no longer a part of our lives. As a pleasant and productive result of this self-rehabilitation, Holmes was more cooperative and insightful than usual as we spent a considerable portion of the year editing my notes on the adventures of the previous year, until our encounter with the so-called Sussex vampire. Of course there were occasions when Scotland Yard would seek his advice on one matter or another, but these were minor contributions that only served to guide the Metropolitan Police in their procedures and did not rise to the status of a worthy Sherlock Holmes adventure.

Abberline kept us informed on Chapman's activities throughout the year. For a time, Chapman and Mary successfully operated the barbershop, Mary playing piano while Chapman serviced the customers. He never abated his nocturnal activities and as a consequence, the business began to fail. Chapman seemed to blame the downturn of events on Mary who, according to observations made by Abberline's agents, began to show evidence of physical abuse. With the failure of the shop, Chapman and Mary moved back to London, whereupon he began to manage the Prince of Wales Pub in Bartholomew Street, with lodgings above the business.

Just after Christmas of 1897, Abberline came to report that following a protracted illness, Mary Spink had died Christmas Day. Holmes's interest was piqued when Abberline stated that Mary had no sooner expired when Chapman proceeded downstairs so as to open the pub for business as usual.

"Abberline, I believe that this suspicious nonchalance in the face of his wife's passing calls for some investigation on our part, especially when we consider the nature of the individual in question," said Holmes in a manner that can only be described as sublime understatement.

Abberline agreed and soon we were on our way to Bartholomew Square, where we found that the Prince of Wales Pub to be closed for an unknown reason. Inquiring at a number of neighbouring buildings, we found a woman who was willing to speak to us once we had identified ourselves. Mrs. Annie Helsdown was duly impressed with Inspector Abberline and perhaps more so with Mr. Sherlock Holmes and consequently could not have been more helpful.

"Oh it was very sad, indeed gentlemen, Mrs. Chapman dying the way she did. I've known them since they came here in August. Thing is, she were the picture of health when they moved in and then things started happening."

"What do you mean?" I asked.

"I'm not one to tell tales but, some nights even from our rooms next door, I could hear them arguing real loud like, and she'd cry out like she'd been hit. Next day I might see her and she'd have these marks like bruises on her. I'd ask her if I could help, but she told me everything was fine, that they just had a little fight and it was her fault and she'd be fine."

"Holmes," I said, "does this remind you of poor Lucy?"

"It does indeed, Watson. What happened next, Mrs. Helsdown?"

"Well, she just got real sick, didn't she? It was all of a sudden like and she just kept getting sicker and sicker. Couldn't keep anything in her. I tried to help out and offered to look in on her and maybe fix her something to eat. But Mr. Chapman, he was an odd one, he was. He told me don't bother, that he was looking after Mary and was giving her the proper medicine. The way he said it let me know I wasn't welcome. Tell you the truth, he scared me. Anyway, I saw her the day before she died and she weren't nothing but skin and bones. I don't know what that medicine was that he were giving her, but it weren't no help to her, that's for sure."

We commended Mrs. Helsdown, thanked for her help, offered her a shilling for her trouble, bade her farewell and made our way back to Baker Street. Once there, we had a conversation as to what we had learned. I spoke first. "I believe that we are in agreement that our Mr. Chapman is more than an odd one, as Mrs. Helsdown would put it."

"Indeed," said Abberline. "It would appear that Mrs. Helsdown is as close as we have come to an eye-witness in the matter of Mr. Chapman."

"Yes," said Holmes, "but she is quite simply not an eye-witness and all that she told us today could only be construed as hearsay conjecture. We would not be any better than she, if we were to give it any more weight than that in the way of proof. However, Watson, you made the observation of the similarity between Chapman's treatment of Mary Spink and that of Lucy and Annie. It is highly suggestive, albeit circumstantial, that this is our man. I would remind you that circumstantial evidence is a very tricky thing. It is a capital mistake to theorise before you have all the evidence. It biases the judgement. That being said, all indications are that we are on the correct path. We can only hope that our investigations will bear fruit before another atrocity is perpetrated. It would be of immeasurable help if we were to ascertain just what medicines Mr. Chapman had been giving to his wife."

"I quite agree with you, Holmes," said Abberline. "In addition to continued surveillance, I shall have my men make inquiries as to a possible source of said medicines."

"Excellent, my dear fellow. I only hope that we are able to make rapid progress."

Part II

Chapter Four

In January of 1898, Abberline brought us news that Chapman, barely weeks after his wife's demise, had hired one Bessie Taylor, an experienced barmaid, to work with him at The Prince of Wales. What transformed this business adjustment into an act of callousness was the fact that the couple soon started living together, with Bessie sharing Chapman's marriage bed.

In due course, Abberline was approached by Mrs. Helsdown and other neighbours who registered complaints as to Chapman's abusive public treatment of Bessie and that they had noticed a series of bruises which Bessie tried, with minimal success, to disguise by taking the somewhat radical step of applying zinc oxide. According to Abberline, Chapman became aware of his neighbour's concern and thus in the summer, Chapman once more fled London, leaving the threat of controversy behind, to take over the running of The Grapes Pub in Hertfordshire. It was during this time that Holmes and I were occupied with the affair of the demented Josiah Amberley as well as the fascinating episode of the dancing men. Because of this, we had to rely on the accuracy of Abberline's reports from the countryside to keep us informed of developments in the case.

Abberline assured us that he would assign agents in Hertfordshire to report on the conduct and activities of Chapman and his new common-law wife. Throughout the year, business at The Grapes was barely fruitful, which apparently served to exacerbate the less cordial aspects of Chapman's behaviour. His mistreatment of Bessie increased in its regularity until finally at the turn of 1899, Chapman sold The Grapes, uprooted Bessie, who was also now suffering from severe dental troubles, and together they moved back to London, where in the spring, Chapman was able to secure The Monument Public House in Union Street, Southwark, one of the poorer districts in London. It was within an hour's walk across the Thames to Whitechapel, with which it shared similar characteristics.

The year 1899 also had Holmes and myself involved in an adventure dealing with the demise of the notorious king of the blackmailers: Charles Augustus Milverton, during which we were nearly apprehended for the destruction of certain compromising papers, the publication of which would have brought undue harm to certain innocent parties. Once we had concluded that business, we turned our attention once again to Mr. George Chapman.

We paid several visits to The Monument over following months and found things to be all above board. Bessie and George seemed to have resolved whatever differences had plagued them in Hertfordshire. There having been no out-of-the-ordinary activities on the part of Chapman for months running, with the exception of his nightly rambles, Abberline suggested that he reduce the intensity of his surveillance. We agreed that he might do well to devote more of his time to other cases in his supervisory position as a Pinkerton operative, but that it was imperative that the Chapman surveillance should not be curtailed entirely. "After all," said Holmes, "we have proceeded thus far on your initial conviction of Chapman being the Whitechapel fiend. I should think that what we have learned to this point would do nothing but increase that conviction within you, just as it has within Watson and myself."

"Of course," said Abberline, "of course. I was merely suggesting that we diminish our intensity of surveillance while intensifying that most invaluable tenet of investigation and deduction: patience."

Holmes gave a short laugh, "Well done, Abberline, you've held me to my own theory and of course you are quite right. Patience it is, then. We will prevail but it will take some time, for the man is careful. I hope not too careful."

I should point out that during the millennial year of 1900, in addition to attention being paid to the events of the Second Boer War in South Africa and the Boxer Rebellion in China, Holmes and I found ourselves in two adventures of note: the curious case of the black pearl of the Borgias as well as solving the problem of the matching revolvers of the Thor Bridge mystery. To be sure, Abberline kept us apprised of the situation at The Monument Pub. All appeared to be reasonably well. Bessie had become active in church activities while her husband did not behave out of the ordinary. Though his nocturnal wanderings had seemed to have increased, this might have been due to a downturn in business, as in the past.

In early December, Holmes and I conducted another investigatory trip to Southwark. We were careful so as not to confront Chapman, but we observed Bessie to be much changed in appearance since we had last seen her. It was enough to give us concern. Through Abberline, we were made aware of one Martha Stevens, a nurse who resided in Union Street, hard by The Monument. We met her outside her residence.

"Mrs. Stevens, I am Sherlock Holmes, this is my associate Dr. Watson. Inspector Abberline informed us that you have some concerns about the well-being of Mrs. Chapman."

"Yes sir, I do," said Mrs. Stevens. "Mrs. Chapman, Bessie that is, had gone into hospital for some extended treatment for an abscess in her mouth. From my conversations with Dr. Stoker, who saw to her, the procedure was successful and he had discharged her to her husband's care with instructions to administer certain medicines."

"That all seems quite proper," I said.

"That is what I thought, Doctor, but I have begun to have my doubts."

"How so?"

"Since my dear husband passed on a year ago, I have frequented The Monument Pub on a regular basis and become quite close to Bessie. I noticed that since her return from treatment in hospital, she has begun to lose weight at a considerable pace. She often complains of stomach ailments, nausea and the inability to retain food. I expressed to Mr. Chapman my willingness to look after and care for Bessie in my capacity as a nurse. He agreed to this, but when I offered to administer the medicines as ordered by Dr. Stoker, he became quite angry. He said that he had been trained as a junior surgeon and was more qualified than I to administer medicine and that he would thank me to simply concern myself with Bessie's physical comfort and cleanliness."

Holmes and I exchanged glances with Abberline at the thought of Chapman's insistence on ministering to his wife to the exclusion of outside help.

"Let me ask you, Nurse Stevens, does Chapman offer her any liquid nourishment?"

"You mean like water? Yes of course he does as she often complains of a terrible thirst, but he also provides her with brandy on a regular basis."

Again we exchanged looks.

"Thank you, Mrs. Stevens, you have been most helpful, indeed."

"I am glad to help," she said. "Maybe it's nothing but I just don't feel comfortable with that Mr. Chapman."

"In my opinion, Nurse Stevens," said Holmes as we began to walk away, "your intuition is well-placed and should be heeded. Thank you again for your help."

As we were near Southwark Station, we were able to hail a Clarence for the ride back to Baker Street. "I believe," said Holmes, "that we are hot on the trail. We must find out what Chapman has been giving to that poor woman."

"Really, Holmes," I said, "why can't we simply ask Dr. Stoker?"

"My dear Watson. I am surprised that you have such little confidence in me after all these years. Of course we can ask Dr. Stoker what he prescribed, but I can assure you that we would find nothing that would prove harmful to his patient. Rather it is what Chapman has been adding to the medicine or to the brandy for that matter, which can prove to be an excellent guise for any number of poisons. Abberline, you have not had any luck locating a likely source among various chemists, have you?"

"Alas, no, Holmes, but my men are still searching."

"You may want to expand your area of inquiry," said Holmes, "and search under the name Klosowski as well as that of Chapman. The answer is certain to provide the key to the solution and the proof that we seek."

The month of January, 1901 brought nationwide sorrow in that Her Majesty the Queen passed away on the 22nd of the month. As a result, it was difficult to pursue our investigation with any degree of efficiency due to a consolidation of all activities and attention, public and private, on the royal tragedy.

In February, we were finally able to secure a meeting with Dr. Stoker who assured us that he had consulted with colleagues as to the treatment of Bessie Taylor. They had jointly reached the conclusion that she was suffering from a form of consumption and that the most they could do was to attempt to relieve her pain and fever by prescribing certain medications including morphine and opium and finally the newly approved drug phenacetin. Despite the ministrations performed on a regular basis by Chapman, Bessie continued her physical decline, as indicated by violent and constant regurgitation as well as flux, to the point where, according to Nurse Stevens, she could not have weighed seven stone by the time she expired on the 13th of February. The cause of death was listed as exhaustion and intestinal obstruction.

Holmes was nearly beside himself with frustration and, I must confess, no small amount of aggravation, at the inability of Abberline and his minions to make any progress in their inquiries. It was obvious to him that a foreign substance had been introduced to Bessie, and just as likely to the prior Mrs. Chapman, which blocked or negated the efficacy of the prescribed medications.

"Would that Wiggins and my Baker Street Irregulars had not grown to maturity," cried Holmes in a fit of anguish. "They would surely have by now identified the poison with which he dispatched his last two wives and whence it was obtained."

"We are agreed then that it was poison that was used?" Abberline asked.

"My dear Abberline," said Holmes in a somewhat conciliatory manner, "it was most assuredly poison and it was utilised on both victims. Over a period of time, both wives experienced exactly the same symptoms, consisting of extended occurrences of nausea, elimination, and painful retching.

"If you recall, in reference to the original Ripper murders, I suggested that the perpetrator had a lust not only for power but for a perverted sexual gratification."

"Yes, but," said Abberline, "these deaths have not been marked by mutilation of any sort unlike those of the Whitechapel victims."

"You are perfectly correct in that Abberline however, the forced length of the decline in the health of the wives while being tended to by Chapman – who refused to let anyone else minister to the women – logically leads one to the understanding that Chapman was in full control of the descent. One of two other factors may also come into play. Contrary to popular belief, which has stymied any number of criminal investigations in the past, is the fact that successful criminals can—and often do, change their methods of operation in order to avoid detection. This is not at all farfetched when one considers Chapman's craftiness, sense of self-preservation and feeling of superiority. It is also entirely possible that Chapman had reached the point of satiation as far as blood lust is concerned and his perversion had been redirected to that of emetophilia which is, to be quite blunt sexual arousal achieved by watching someone regurgitate."

"Really Holmes," said Abberline, "I don't think…"

"It really doesn't matter what you think, Abberline," said Holmes in as kindly a manner as he could muster. "This is not about thinking or surmising on any of our parts." he explained. "It is about the collection and examination of evidence no matter how far fetched it may seem to you or me or Watson."

"I understand, Holmes," Abberline said. "And I do concur with you in this respect; though the incentive may change, the fiendishness is not eradicated."

"Certainly, Abberline, certainly. But I must add that though postmortems would be invaluable in our investigation, none appears to be forthcoming, since causes of death have already been ascribed and recorded. Therefore, we are left with intensifying our surveillance and broadening our search for the source of Chapman's poison. Agreed?"

"Agreed," said Abberline resignedly as he could not but follow Holmes' indisputable logic and path of reasoning. I of course agreed while foreseeing yet another extended period of patience.

Part II
Chapter Five

Abberline kept up his vigil throughout the early part of 1901. Chapman continued to operate The Monument Pub, but did not appear to be particularly efficient in doing so, again perhaps due to his late night, at times all-night, distressing activities. These continued to the point whereupon some days he did not open for business at all. This was of some concern only in so far as that it might predicate some criminal act on the part of Chapman in order to mitigate the damage, but thus far no crime had been committed.

In May, Holmes and I ventured to Northern England to investigate the kidnapping of a young lord at an exclusive preparatory school. Holmes handily solved the case in a matter of two days by piecing together some apparently desultory evidence and received a handsome fee for his efforts.

Abberline reported to us that in August, in an apparent effort to stave off business failure, Chapman had hired a young girl named Maud Marsh who, at age eighteen, was an experienced barmaid.

"I fear," said Holmes. "that young Mistress Marsh has placed herself in harm's way."

"Initially, I had a similar thought," said Abberline, "save for the fact that she was engaged for the position when

Chapman answered an advertisement in a newspaper that Maud had placed seeking employment. When she went to The Monument to be interviewed, she was accompanied by her mother and one of her sisters. It would appear that the Marsh family is a respectable one that takes an interest in their young daughter's well-being."

"I certainly hope that your optimism is not misplaced. Taking into consideration the results of Chapman's questionable conjugal relationships in the past, we are duty-bound to remain on high alert. I would remind you that we are dealing with an extremely cunning individual and as such, I implore you not to lessen your surveillance. I tell you, Abberline, this fiend has not finished his work, nor have we ours."

"I assure you, Holmes, Watson, that my charges and I are up to the challenge. Besides, I think with Maud's family in close touch, Chapman would be foolish to attempt anything under the conditions that exist at this moment, and we all know that Chapman is hardly foolish."

The ensuing weeks proved Abberline accurate in that nothing unexpected transpired. Maud's family, including her father, visited often and seemed to be content with the burgeoning closeness between Chapman and their daughter.

In the middle of October, Abberline brought us the news that Chapman and Maud were married.

"Married! Again? Ha!" I cried. "Isn't Chapman still wed to Lucy?"

"Indeed, he is," said Abberline, "but that seems to make no difference to him, and I would be much surprised if Maud had any indication of the fact."

"But her parents," I said.

"Her parents are under the impression that Chapman is a widower, which is true in a common-law sense, so to speak. In addition, they were only recently presented with the announcement of the marriage as a fait accompli."

"Fascinating," said Holmes. "Chapman has taken the first step again on his well-trodden trail of treachery. Of course, due to the presence of Maud's family, he has had to approach this differently. As we have seen from the progress of the relationship from August until now, he has completely taken in her relatives and put them at their ease, which, I am afraid, throws open the gate to further tragedy."

By virtue of the diligence of Abberline and his men, we learned that despite all efforts, The Monument Pub was in dire financial straits and that the lease on the establishment was about to expire. Therefore, it came as no great surprise when on the 10th of December, Abberline announced that there had been a fire on the premises just the night before and that it had been fairly destroyed. Of course neither Holmes, Abberline nor myself believed for one moment that this was an accident. We were certain that this had been a ploy on Chapman's part to collect on an insurance policy he had taken out just one month previous. This prompted a trip to Union Street so that we might examine the damage. Abberline went with us.

The structure itself, though somewhat gutted, still stood. Taking advantage of Abberline's good relationship with the Metropolitan Police, we were able to enter and examine what was left of The Monument. Our tour of the building was cut short when Holmes turned to us and said, "That's quite enough. We've seen what we needed to see." Luckily, Abberline had thought to have our cab linger at the scene, so we remounted and instructed the driver to return us to Baker Street.

Once in the cab, I anticipated Abberline's question when I asked Holmes what he meant by having seen what we had to see.

"Ah Watson, old fellow, once again you see but you do not observe."

"I don't understand. There was nothing there to see."

"Exactly," said Holmes, "nothing, no chairs, no tables, no customary accoutrements of a public house save the bar, which was hardly damaged since the fire was somewhat contained to the cellar."

"What do you make of it, Holmes?" I asked.

"Unless I am wrong, which of course I am not, our friend Mr. Chapman was so well-prepared for the fire, he removed all the furnishing to another location to save them from the conflagration, which he then proceeded to initiate in the cellar."

"So you think it was arson?" asked Abberline.

"I am sure of it," said Holmes. "Because of a lack of capital and the upcoming termination of his lease, Chapman decided to mitigate his situation by defrauding the insurance company and collecting on a tragic fire which he himself had set. I would have expected nothing less from him. It is yet another indication of his, shall we say, questionable grasp of legality, if not morality in general. Fortunately for us and the insurers and unfortunately for Mr. Chapman, his strategy, tactics as well as his incendiary skills leave something to be desired. He is getting careless, and dare I say, sloppy in his contrivances."

"Indeed," said Abberline. "Since the name of the pub's insurer is a matter of public record, it shall be my pleasure to alert that company as to our findings and our suspicions. I feel certain that the insurer will want to conduct its own investigation, because it is my understanding that insurers frown upon making payments in cases of arson when said crime was possibly committed by the insured."

"Quite so," said Holmes with a somewhat sinister chuckle.

"If I may," I said, "it will be quite interesting to see how Chapman handles this turn of events."

We did not have long to wait.

Part II

Chapter Six

Shortly before Christmas, Abberline surprised us with the news that somehow, some way, Chapman had secured tenure of a larger and rather more respectable public house called The Crown in Borough High Street in London. Located hard by Guy's Hospital, The Crown was regularly frequented by medical students. Chapman was to assume the duties as publican shortly after the first of the year.

"He certainly has a talent for wresting some sort of victory from the jaws of imminent defeat," I said.

"He does that," said Holmes, "but I wonder for how much longer. From this development, we can only conclude that Chapman did not realise his anticipated windfall from the insurance company, correct?"

"That is absolutely correct, Holmes. As I learned from the insurance company, acting upon the information we provided them, they conducted an investigation and concluded that the fire was indeed a case of arson under ambiguous circumstances, which conclusion was supported by a follow-up police investigation."

"Hmm," said Holmes, "I gather from Chapman's relocation that he was not implicated."

"He was not."

"Of course not," Holmes continued, "he is far too clever to leave any self-incriminating evidence at the scene of a crime. Tell me, Abberline, how did Chapman explain the detail that the pub was devoid of furniture at the time of the fire?"

"Ah, yes, that detail. He explained that he had been in the process of making improvements to the establishment when the fire broke out and that if it was arson, as contended, it must have been the act of a disgruntled customer."

"Of course,' said Holmes as he crossed the room to the mantelpiece and his slipper of tobacco.

"He appealed to the company to rescind its refusal of compensation, but the appeal was, as you see, turned down."

"It is my sincere hope," said Holmes while lighting his pipe, "that this circumstance is merely the introduction to his downfall and apprehension: the beginning of his end, as it were."

For the first few months of the year 1902, Abberline's efforts did not yield any information about Chapman's habits that diverged from or added to that of which we were already aware. He still made his nightly patrols in debauchery and the treatment of his new wife mirrored that of his treatment of his three previous female companions. We feared that this did not bode well for young Maud Marsh.

During the months of May, June, July, and August, our attention was focused on a series of cases which included the matter of Sir Robert Norberton and Shoscombe Prince, as well as the peculiar incidents of the three Garridebs. Lastly the convoluted case of the disappearance of Lady Frances Carfax, took me to Switzerland, Germany and France, where I was nearly strangled in an altercation. Returning to Baker Street, I was understandably exhausted. Accordingly I was more than glad to accept Holmes' invitation to accompany him to inspect one of two estates he had been considering for his eventual retirement.

The excursion to the South Downs in Sussex was an example of the new, yet oddly appropriate idiom: just what the doctor ordered. With an extraordinary view of the Channel, I could not imagine a more peaceful setting in which Holmes might spend his post-detective years. It was so serene and rejuvenating that we extended our stay to a fortnight before returning to Baker Street.

We had arrived back in London when we learned that the new Mrs. Chapman had been stricken with an unidentified illness, which caused her to run a temperature, become sick to her stomach, unable to hold nourishment, excessively thirsty, and to suffer abdominal pains. Her parents, over Chapman's objections, insisted that she be admitted to Guy's Hospital. Although Chapman claimed to be more than capable of caring for Maud himself, professional treatment improved her condition to the point where she was discharged, ironically, to her husband's care.

September brought Holmes and myself two more cases that called for immediate attention. One of these involved a murderous scoundrel who, having arranged for Holmes to be beaten by hired thugs, finally received his comeuppance by way of a face full of vitriol flung by one of the women he had wronged. The other, while considerably less dangerous to either Holmes or myself, did involve coming to grips with a certain, secret criminal organisation. The adventure came to a conclusion and justice was served. However, it did mark the end of our long and fruitful association with Inspector Tobias Gregson of Scotland Yard.

At the conclusion of these undertakings, Holmes prevailed upon me once again to accompany him to inspect the second of his potential retirement homes, which was located near East Hill in Hastings. The Chapman investigation appeared calm at the moment and Abberline's forces, we felt, were capable of carrying out their simple surveillance duties. For her part, Maud seemed to be on the road to recovery.

With events calmed for the time being, I took it upon myself to insist upon a postponement of the Hastings trip. At the beginning of October, I committed what Holmes referred to as "the only selfish act I can recall in our relationship"; I married for a third time. The courtship, though intense and determined, was one of fits and starts due, I confess, to the nature of my activities. While expressing an understanding of my relationship with Mr. Sherlock Holmes, my new bride was not as lenient with me as had been Constance and Mary. She felt that a husband's place was in his home with his wife, and a doctor's place, in his surgery. Consequently, I relocated with her to Queen Anne Street and compromises were reached on both sides of the equation.

In late October therefore, I felt comfortable enough to engage a first-class compartment for Holmes and myself for the two-hour train journey from Charing Cross to Hastings Station. Once there, Holmes seemed a bit distracted and did not appear to be anxious to leave the metropolitan area.

"I say, Holmes, are you going to have me examine your proposed retirement villa or are you not?"

"All in good time, Watson, all in good time." He then proceeded to lead me on an exploratory tour of town centre.

We had been conducting this perambulation for nearly an hour when I finally tired of feigning interest and said, "Really, Holmes, are we to wander about like this all day? You know I rarely complain, but I am afraid this gallivant has awakened the effects of my old war wound."

"Oh my dear fellow, I am sincerely sorry. And I must make a confession. Having you inspect my proposed retirement villa was merely a handy excuse to get you to accompany me here. I knew that you would be anxious to see where I might spend my elder years. I also knew that you would be less anxious to traipse around Hastings in an exercise that could well prove futile."

"What on Earth are you talking about, Holmes?"

"I am sure you recall that Chapman had operated a number of tonsoriums here in Hastings."

"Certainly I recall."

"It occurred to me that Abberline never mentioned that his agents had searched the Hastings area for a source of a substance that Chapman may have used to poison his victims. No doubt you agree, that was a dangerous oversight. Consequently, I thought that we might perform that duty ourselves."

"Really Holmes, I am disappointed that you have so little confidence in me that you'd have to resort to subterfuge to…"

"Watson, please. I assure you that my confidence in you is unwavering. As I have told you in the past, you are more than my Boswell. You are my indispensable partner and I would never do anything to harm you or to do you a disservice. The reasons for my actions were two-fold: I realised that our last adventure taxed you more than usual, indeed perhaps more than was necessary, and that an outing to the shore would be just what was needed to restore you to full vitality. Had I been forthright with you on my real reason for the trip, I was afraid you would have pleaded fatigue and demurred. Therefore, I employed the ruse."

"Holmes, believe me when I say that I am just as anxious as yourself to put this case to rest. I would not have baulked at the challenge."

"I realise that now Watson, and I am truly sorry."

"Of course. Now tell me: what is the second reason?"

"If I am not mistaken, and of course I am not, it was imperative that you make this trip with me. As you now know, we are in search of the source of the poison with which we believe Chapman committed his murders. The most obvious source for things such as that is a chemist's shop. It is true, is it not, that chemists are reluctant to discuss their clientele with individuals outside their profession?"

I felt a surge of pride as I began to understand Holmes' reasoning. "Yes that is true," I said, "with the exception of members of the medical profession, of which I am one."

"You are indeed," said Holmes, "and it is my belief that should we be able to locate an amenable chemist, you might avail yourself of your standing as a medical doctor, not to mention your considerable talents as an actor, that you so ably demonstrated in the matter of the murderous Baron Gruner, to make inquiries regarding a certain patient of yours about whom you've had grave concerns. What do you say to that?"

"What I must say, Holmes, is that your deviousness is on a par with your genius."

"Well?"

"My good man, even as we stand here and waste time, my concern over the well-being of my patient only grows. Let us continue our quest with all due speed," I said with a smile as Holmes clapped me on the shoulder.

We set off at a goodly clip, the nagging pains from my old wounds having miraculously disappeared. As we turned the corner to High Street, Holmes looked to the left, while I looked straight ahead and came to an abrupt stop. "Hello," I said, "what have we here?" Across the way, attached to the front of the building at number 231 High Street was a sign that read "W. Davidson – Chemist".

"I believe," said Holmes, "that we have discovered a showcase where you might exercise your thespian abilities."

"So we have," I said, as we crossed the street and entered the establishment.

Announced by a bell suspended over the door, we were greeted by the familiar chemical smell of all chemist shops, with the underlying pungent odour of sulphur. On shelves below a glass-topped counter was the usual display of nostrums, elixirs and patent medicines, including vials of liquid cocaine toward which, I am proud to say, Holmes gave a derisive sniff. As we examined the vast array of small wooden files, each bearing the name of a chemical on the wall behind the counter, a short, rather untidy, bespectacled man emerged through a curtain from the back room and greeted us. "Good day, gentlemen. How may I be of assistance?"

"Good day to you, sir," I said. "Are you the chemist?"

"That I am, sir. William Davidson at your service. Now, may I help you?"

"I sincerely hope so. I am Dr. John H Watson, MD," I said as I proffered one of my visiting cards, the habit of carrying which I had retained since I had first established my practice. "This is my associate Mr. Sherrinford," I said as I gestured to Holmes.

"I see," said Mr. Davidson as he read my card. "You gentlemen are a long way from London. Is this a social call? On holiday, perhaps?"

"I'm afraid not," I said. "Our visit is on more of a professional nature."

"Ah then, please enlighten me."

"I am quite concerned about the well-being of a patient of mine who resided in Hastings for a time, a Mr. George Chapman. He may have had occasion to avail himself of your services."

"Of course, of course! George Chapman. He was a barber and operated a shop with his wife in George Street."

"I'm surprised that you remembered him so quickly. It must be over three years ago that he lived here."

"Oh, it is easily that," said Davidson, "but they stood out, him and his wife, didn't they? She, her name was Mary, I believe, would play piano while George did the honours on the customers. It was very enjoyable. I frequented the shop on a regular basis. Then, something happened, don't you know, and they moved back to London. Financial trouble I heard. Of course that's where you must have come across him. Anyway, he has returned several times through the past years to purchase more of his original order. His wife's constitution was never the best, so it seems, and I fear that her condition has not improved. He was here not a month ago and requested the same remedy."

Holmes could hardly contain himself, "Which was?"

"Well, I'm trying to be delicate here, Doctor. Tartar emetic." He then paused, "It is somewhat embarrassing to speak of this, for as you know, tartar emetic is often used in the treatment of the French disease, of which Chapman's wife was a victim, or so I was led to believe. What a shame. The poor man. I feel sorry for him, being so devoted and all."

"Devoted, yes quite so," I said.

"In fact," Davidson continued, "I have never seen a man quite so devoted. It certainly is a sad thing to have a life so beset by such tribulations. Such a pity indeed. I thought it odd, Doctor, that Mr. Chapman would travel to Hastings to resupply himself of the medicine, don't you know? Plenty of chemists in London. But then again, when you consider the nature of his wife's affliction, he probably wanted to spare her and himself the public embarrassment. So he thought it wiser to do his shopping, so to speak, out of town and in a place he felt safe and out of harm's way, if you see what I mean."

Holmes could barely contain himself as he exited the shop and left me to thank Mr. Davidson for his cooperation. Utilising the Holmesian device of a placating phrase of departure, I said, "Thank you Mr. Davidson. You have been most helpful. Your information will be of immeasurable aid to ease Mr. Chapman's pain as well as that of his poor wife."

Exiting the shop, I found Holmes pacing back and forth. "Watson! Congratulations on your performance!"

I was taken aback. "It was hardly a performance, Holmes. I am a physician after all."

"Certainly, my dear fellow, certainly. I was referring to the genuine concern you exhibited regarding the well-being of poor Mr. Chapman. Excellent job! Had I not known better, I could have sworn you were sincere! I could not have done better myself."

"Why thank you, Holmes. That is high praise coming from you."

"Yes, well now do you realise what you have accomplished? You have uncovered the key to the solution of our investigation, the factor that confirms the circumstantial evidence we have amassed. I agree with Mr. Davidson that tartar emetic may, in some cases, be used as a treatment for the French disease. In addition, considering Chapman's nocturnal activities, it is possible that his wife or wives might well have contracted the affliction from him, yet I do not, for one instant, believe it to be so in this matter.

"I am convinced that Chapman is Jack the Ripper, that he murdered two of his wives and that he did it by way of poison."

"I am in full agreement with you, Holmes. As we both know, an emetic is a substance used to induce vomiting, and that further, tartar emetic is the shortened version of antimony potassium tartrate and that it is indeed quite poisonous under many conditions."

"That's it exactly, Watson. Applications of the substance induce regurgitation. Prolonged application produces prolonged regurgitation, severe weight loss and ultimately, death. Such was the case with Chapman's two previous wives.

"Moreover, Watson, the information we've received from Mr. Davidson gives us more insight regarding the nature of our Mr. Chapman. In reference to Chapman's need for the medicine, he mentioned Chapman's wife, in the singular. This would indicate that he assumed that Chapman had the same wife over the years and that her indelicate behaviour did not abate over that time, which occasioned the recurrence of the pox, which in turn occasioned Chapman's trips to avail himself of Mr. Davidson's elixir."

"Yes, Holmes, but we already know that Chapman is a malignancy on humanity. Does this tell us something further?"

"It most certainly does, Watson, old fellow. It proves that there is not one redeeming facet to Chapman's character. There is nothing, no method so vile, that he would not stoop to use to achieve his ends. What he has done is to infer, invent if you will, his wife's questionable character in order to garner sympathy from and take advantage of an unsuspecting, rather weak-minded chemist, who assumed the worst about the woman in question and pitied the poor, put upon, long-suffering husband.

"What Chapman has done is to soil his wife's reputation to enable him to purchase the mechanism of her demise. In essence, he arranged for both of his wives to pay with their reputations for their own deaths and judging from his recent visit to Mr. Davidson, the death of wife number three is waiting in the wings for its entrance."

"My word, Holmes! This creature is quite simply evil incarnate and must be stopped! It is imperative!"

"It is that, Watson. Once more, the game is afoot. We must alert Abberline to our discovery as quickly as we can return to London"

"Holmes, perhaps we might telegraph first, don't you think?"

"Of course you are right, Watson. My word, you will make a detective yet. Oh and I apologise, Watson, but your inspection of my proposed estate will have to wait until another time. Come quickly, we can avail ourselves of the telegraph office at Hastings Station."

Part II

Chapter Seven

Arriving back at Charing Cross in the late afternoon of October 22nd, we were met on the platform by an obviously dejected Abberline, who approached us before we could approach him. "Holmes, Watson, I am most glad you are back but I fear you are too late for the poor girl. Young Maud passed away at half-past noon this day."

"That is indeed unfortunate, Abberline," said Holmes, "would that we might have returned sooner. It is truly a shame. However, our work is far from finished. Though we are too late for poor Maud, perhaps by her death she may yet be of inestimable help to see that justice is served. Tell me: where did she die?"

"In her bed in her rooms above The Crown Public House."

"Is her body still there?"

"I believe it is."

"Capital! We must proceed straight away to The Crown and investigate the premises without delay."

Abberline had thought to retain the use of a growler and in short order we were on our way to Southwark. On the way, Abberline apprised us of the recent history of events that had led to the demise of the late Maud Marsh Chapman.

"As you are aware, dating back nearly to the time she first became involved with Chapman, Maud has not been in the best of health. Numerous hospital stays, examinations, and ministrations by several doctors have provided her relief for only short periods of time. Hope would be built up for a panacea only to be dashed by a relapse."

"You mentioned several doctors," I said. "Could you provide me with some names?"

Abberline consulted a small notebook which he retrieved from his coat pocket. "There was a Doctor Stoker, whom you may recall treated the previous Mrs. Chapman, who also passed away. He was followed by Doctors Sunderland, Cotter, Grapel and Thorpe."

"Yes, I am familiar with those gentlemen. They are all brothers of mine in the medical profession. However, it is an unfortunate matter of fact that some brothers are of a lesser stature than others. With the possible exception of Doctor Grapel, I would place the others in the category of lesser stature."

"It is interesting that you should say that, Dr. Watson, because their diagnoses differ wildly. Dr. Sunderland claimed that Maud was experiencing severe female complaints. Dr. Cotter diagnosed ptomaine poisoning, while Dr. Thorpe announced that this was simply a case of hysteria. Dr. Stoker offered no opinion and Dr. Grapel has thus far remained ominously close-mouthed."

"I see. Please continue," Holmes urged.

"Events took an intriguing turn yesterday when Mrs. Marsh, that is to say, Maud's mother, allowed as she had been growing more and more suspicious regarding her daughter's treatments. She was concerned to the point where she asked Dr. Stoker to secure further medical advice. Stoker readily complied and called in his colleague, Dr. Grapel. At my request, they are standing by at The Crown awaiting our arrival."

Presently, our carriage stopped in front of the pub. Standing at some distance from the doctors were two gentlemen I did not recognize. Alighting from the cab, Abberline took the initiative and introduced us to two of his former Scotland Yard associates: Chief Inspector George Godley and Inspector Arthur Neil."

"Gentlemen," said Holmes, "I am pleased to make your acquaintance, but I must confess it is a bit surprising to find you here."

"Oh not so surprising, Mr. Holmes," said CI Godley. "When you consider that we have been among the foremost supporters of Abberline's theories through thick and thin and have shared his fixation with Mr. Chapman for some years now."

"In that case, gentlemen, you are most welcome. Watson and I look forward to availing ourselves of your professional services before long, I should think. Don't you agree Watson?"

"Indeed I do, Holmes, indeed I do. Now, allow me to introduce Doctors Grapel and Stoker."

"Ah yes, gentlemen. I am honoured to make your acquaintance. Dr. Watson has spoken highly of you both. Now, what can you tell me of your conclusions regarding Mrs. Chapman?"

"You realise, Mr. Holmes," said Dr. Stoker, "that we are but the latest of a number of physicians called in on this case, do you not?"

"I do."

"And you must understand that although we have all received similar training, our opinions may diverge on occasion?"

"Yes, I have often found that to be the case."

"Well then," continued Stoker, "only yesterday morning, I attended to Mrs. Chapman and found her to be semi-comatose but, curiously, with a strong heart and a quick pulse. At the behest of Mrs. Marsh, Grapel accompanied me here last evening. The young woman was awake, somewhat alert and looked better than she had earlier in the day. I spoke to her husband about this and offered my opinion that she was suffering from a severe case of gastroenteritis and that in all probability, with proper treatment, she would recover in due time. That declaration elicited a most odd response from Mr. Chapman."

"Oh?"

"Quite inexplicably he grew angry and announced that he did not think that was the case. Expressing resentment that Dr. Grapel had been called in to consult, he then turned and abruptly left the room. By the time we had returned here today, the poor girl was dead."

"Fascinating," said Holmes.

"Mr, Holmes, if I may?" asked Dr. Grapel.

"Please," said Holmes.

"This is where Dr. Stoker and I had reached distinctly different interpretations. Last evening, I found myself in the uncomfortable opinion of being in agreement with Chapman. Since she had requested my expertise, I took it as my duty to convey my conclusion to Mrs. Marsh. I informed her that in my opinion, her daughter was not suffering from a severe case of gastroenteritis or peritonitis but rather that she was the victim of slow poisoning and that judging by my understanding of the symptoms, this was in fact an incident of arsenic poisoning. Though I could offer her no explanation as to how this was possible, Mrs. Marsh muttered to me that she held a strong notion of exactly how this was possible. As she said this, she glared past me toward Chapman, who hovered over her daughter."

"Most interesting," said Holmes. "Now to eliminate the impossible, I must ask you if to your knowledge, had you or any of your colleagues taken it upon themselves to prescribe arsenic to the patient?"

"Absolutely not, Mr. Holmes," said Dr. Grapel as he drew himself up to his full height and Dr. Stoker shook his head in agreement. "As a matter of course, I consulted with the appropriate physicians at Guy's Hospital as well as other colleagues who had examined Mrs. Chapman. I can attest to the fact that not one of them, nor I for that matter, prescribed arsenic to the unfortunate girl. That includes Dr. Cotter who had diagnosed cancer, for which Dr. Watson can tell you, treatment with arsenic had proven to be effective under certain circumstances. No sir, Mr. Holmes. No arsenic, no purgative of any kind, including antimony wine, I assure you. In fact, from my consultations with the medical staff at Guy's Hospital, all prescribed treatments and medicines have been in the nature of palliative care, such as bismuth powder, phenacetin or opium in order to grant the poor girl some intestinal relief."

At the mention of antimony, Holmes turned toward me and rendered a tight, grim smile. Turning back to the doctors, he said, "One last question, Doctor. Did any of the examinations find any evidence of what is often referred to as the French disease?

"Again, absolutely not, Mr. Holmes. I realise the question is indelicate, but I suppose, all things considered, it must be asked."

"You are quite correct, Doctor. That possibility had to be eliminated. Thank you both. You have been of immense help."

Then he addressed Abberline. "If you will do the honours, Abberline, please lead Watson and myself into the premises so that we might view the body."

Walking into the establishment, Holmes remarked that it was rather curious that in light of what had transpired, the pub was open for business. This was reminiscent of the circumstances surrounding Bessie Taylor's death. As we were crossing the floor to the back stairway which led to the first floor, Abberline was approached by a man who came from behind the bar. He was of average height with thick dark hair, a heavy black moustache, and with his sleeves rolled up, was in the process of drying a glass mug with a towel. "Inspector Abberline, a word if you please."

"No, not at the moment," said Abberline curtly as we made for the door to the stairwell. "I promise I shall deal with you later, sir."

Holmes studied this exchange. As we climbed the stairs, Holmes said, "I take it that was our man."

"It was," said Abberline.

"I thought as much. His eyes had the look of a mad intensity about them, particularly so after your abrupt dismissal. I also noticed the muscular nature of his hands and forearms as he cleaned the glass mug, which to me indicated a strength that was fully capable of throttling someone, operating a pair of barber's shears or performing an impromptu surgery. Little observations, I know, but to the deductive mind, nothing is little."

Arriving at the landing we stopped. Turning to face Abberline and myself, Holmes remarked, "I must say that I find the man's composure bordering on the fantastic if not on the obscene, what with his wife not dead but several hours, he is back fulfilling his responsibilities as publican one floor below where lies his dearly departed."

"Well put, Holmes but even without your deductive powers, I believe that Abberline and I were able to take note of the same somewhat macabre incongruity."

We then crossed the hall and opened the door to poor Maud's bedroom, now her death chamber. Seated at the side of the bed and holding the frail hand and gazing upon the frightfully gaunt face of her daughter was Mrs. Robert Marsh. A constable stood to the right of the door. Abberline softly cleared his throat.

Mrs. Marsh looked up. "Oh, Inspector. I am so glad you're here. I have spoken with Dr. Grapel and he has told me that he suspects that my poor Maud was murdered."

"Yes," said Abberline. "We have also spoken with Dr. Grapel and he told us the same. These men," he gestured toward Holmes and myself "are colleagues who have been working with me and of whom I am certain can be of vital assistance in the matter of Maud's death. Permit me introduce Dr. John Watson and Mr. Sherlock Holmes."

"Dear lady," said Holmes, "please accept our sincere condolences on the unfortunate death of your daughter. I only wish that we might have been able to act earlier so that poor Maud might still be with you."

"Thank you, Mr. Holmes. I wish my husband were here to express his thanks but this morning was taken ill; the stress and strain have been too much for his already weak constitution. He was admitted yesterday to Guy's Hospital, where poor Maudie had been treated."

She began to sob. "I'm so sorry, Mr. Holmes, it's just…"

"No apologies are necessary, I assure you. And I do wish your husband a speedy recovery," said Holmes as he placed a comforting hand on her shoulder.

He paused for a moment and then continued. "Now, please forgive me but I am afraid I must put a series of what may be uncomfortable questions to you, even in this fragile hour of your grief."

"Oh, please proceed, Mr. Holmes, if it will help to make some sense out of this terrible misfortune."

"Very well, Mrs. Marsh. Were you satisfied with the diagnoses given you by the various physicians who attended your daughter?"

"No, sir."

"Did you have suspicions as to the nature of your daughter's illness and why she did not appear to be recovering?"

"Yes, sir."

"Although your daughter is beyond our help now, are you willing to have her participate in an investigation into the matter of our poisoning?"

"I'm sorry, Mr. Holmes, I don't understand"

"What I mean is that it is my understanding that Dr. Grapel indicated to you that your daughter may have been the victim of arsenic poisoning. Is that correct?"

"Yes, sir."

"Mrs. Marsh, based on the results of my investigation, it is my considered opinion that your daughter did not die from arsenic poisoning. I suspect that Maud was the victim of prolonged application of antimony potassium tartrate, which means she was killed by antimony poisoning. What's more, Dr. Watson and I, along with Inspector Abberline, are quite convinced that the poisoning was carried out by her husband, whom you know as George Chapman."

"I don't understand, Mr. Holmes. Whom I know as George Chapman? What do you mean?"

"I mean that under another name, we are convinced that Mr. Chapman has murdered two previous wives by the same method and a number of other women by methods best left unmentioned."

"Oh no! Can this be true?

"I fear that it can be and is true, Mrs. Marsh. Now are you willing to do what must be done in order to bring this fiend to justice?"

"Why yes, of course. What is it?"

"It is necessary that you consent to, dare I say insist on, a full and detailed post mortem to be performed on your daughter so that we might confirm the nature of the poison that was introduced to her. Unless I am in error, which is highly unlikely, in addition to other evidence we have discovered, this would serve to establish Chapman's guilt in the murder of your daughter. It would also animate the call for the disinterment of his prior victims. By granting permission for, indeed your insistence on, the procedure, you would be avenging Maud's death, the death of two likewise innocent young women, and seeing to it that Chapman's murderous rampage is brought to an end."

"I see. Yes, Mr. Holmes, I know I can speak for my husband. We agree completely with your suggestion. In her death, Maud will see to it that justice will be served."

She stood. "Yes, yes indeed."

"Excellent," said Holmes. "Abberline will you see to it?"

"I will Holmes, I shall go and have a word with Chief Inspector Godley, whom I feel certain will agree with our thoughts on the matter. I have no doubt that he will summarily convey our suspicions, and Mrs. Marsh's wishes as to this unnatural death, to the coroner, who in turn shall undoubtedly order an immediate post-mortem,"

"Capital. Mrs. Marsh, may we be of any further assistance to you?"

"No thank you, Mr. Holmes. I am most grateful. My other daughters should be here momentarily. They've just been to visit their father. I'm sure the constable will see to me until then."

"Very well, Mrs. Marsh. Again, our deepest condolences"

With that, Holmes and I went back to the ground floor, where we found Abberline in spirited conversation with Chapman.

"I tell you, Inspector, I insist that Maud's body be removed from here now, tonight!"

"Oh, but I am afraid that is quite impossible Mr. Chapman – or whatever your name is. You see, Mrs. Marsh has requested that a private post mortem be performed. Chief Inspector Godley has been good enough to relay that request to the proper authorities. In light of that, Maud will remain where she is until tomorrow morning, at which point she will be transported to an authorised facility whereupon the procedure will be performed by a team of properly licensed physicians attached to the coroner's office. Until that procedure is completed, no death certificate may be signed."

"That is outrageous, Inspector! As Maud's husband, I have a right to…"

"I beg to differ, sir. Your activities have been under scrutiny for a number of years now and there is some question as to the legitimacy of your present marriage, therefore you have no standing in the matter and no rights as a surviving spouse."

"We shall see about that," Chapman fairly spat at Abberline.

"And to ensure that nothing untoward befalls poor Maud during the night, a constable shall remain stationed at her bedside until relieved when she is removed in the morning."

Leaving Chapman sputtering in anger, Abberline turned away and accompanied Holmes and myself out of the pub.

"My compliments, Abberline," said Holmes with a wry smile, on the exemplary manner in which you conducted that discussion. May we impose upon you to accompany us back to Baker Street where we might indulge in a brandy, for medicinal purposes of course, and discuss the chain of events that have brought us to this point?"

"I should like nothing better, Holmes. As it so happens, I do have some questions regarding your analysis of the matter."

Part III

Chapter One

Mounting Abberline's cab, which he had thought to keep waiting, we proceeded back to Marylebone, crossing the Thames by way of Waterloo Bridge. After we arrived at Baker Street and made our way to Holmes's sitting room, Holmes did the honours and poured us each a brandy, adding soda from the gasogene which was kept on the sideboard.

"Thank you, Holmes," said Abberline as he seated himself on the sofa. "I believe you will understand me," he continued, "when I tell you that this case has had me at my wit's end. These last fourteen years have brought nothing less than total frustration up until today. I believe, sir, we are on the cusp of victory."

"I quite agree with you, Abberline."

"Hear, hear," I toasted, as I sat in a side chair, while with a smile, Holmes crossed to the mantel and his Persian slipper of Arcadia mixture with which he filled his churchwarden, blackened clay pipe.

"Now, Abberline," said Holmes, after he had lit his pipe and taken his first puff, "is there any aspect of the case upon which I might enlighten you?"

"Now that you ask, there are several. Foremost is the fact that over the passage of time, Maud seemed to fluctuate between dire illness and robust activity nearly overnight it would seem. In fact, at one point, Chapman had hired a young woman, Florence Rayner by name, to assist with the operation of the pub. This would have been acceptable had Chapman not begun to make overt advances toward the girl, who was at least somewhat receptive to his attentions. In short order, Maud became aware of these overtures and energetically made the suggestion that Florence might be wise to seek other employment, if she knew what was good for her."

"Remarkable," said Holmes. "Not to appear insensitive, but Maud would have been better off if the situation were reversed."

"Quite so," said Abberline, "but how do you explain this sudden energetic recovery?"

"I can assure you, Abberline, that this and the other recoveries were only temporary and intended by Chapman to be so. The man is crafty, but Watson and I have fairly ascertained his method. Maud's sickness was being induced by Chapman, much as he induced it in his previous wives: very slowly and over a period of time, cumulatively causing discomfort, pain, an inability to retain nourishment in any form, weight loss, weakness, confusion, and ultimately death. The symptoms could conveniently be ascribed to any number of illnesses as they indeed were.

"Abberline, you must consider the man's guile. He utilised hospital treatments and prescribed medicine to draw out the process. The treatments were effective, but they did not negate the presence and accumulation of poison in his victim's body. The administration of toxins were resumed with scarcely any notable diminution of effect and only served to draw out the suffering. Treatments of bismuth powder, opium, and the like served to provide transitory relief to the stomach disorder, severe pain, and suffering caused by the poison. In fact, the poison did not dissipate but remained in her organs. In effect, the continued applications of legitimate treatments offered by the doctors only prolonged poor Maud's agonies. In this, these well-meaning physicians served as unwitting accomplices to Chapman's depredations."

"My word, Holmes! That is simply horrible!"

"Indeed it is, my dear Abberline. I think you will find that it is only one small step from the grotesque to the truly horrible."

"As you say, Holmes," said Abberline as he shakily lifted his glass to take a generous swallow. "I understand the fiend's tactics as you explain them, but with his mental acuity and his obviously treacherous intelligence, he must have had a motive in all this, but for the life of me, I cannot name it – other than the possibility that he simply enjoyed killing."

"I suppose there may be something to that tangentially, Abberline. As you realise, we are not dealing with the everyday professional criminal, whose motives are always centred on profit of one sort or another. No, it is obvious that Chapman does not murder for monetary gain, for even that has some understandable rationale behind it. As Watson and I have discovered, when you have eliminated the impossible, whatever remains, *however improbable*, must be the truth. Therefore, we must conclude that Chapman's motives are singular and very, very personal. I realise that this may be difficult for you to accept, Abberline, but do you recall that I mentioned emetophilia fetish in the case of Bessie Taylor's death?"

"I do indeed, Holmes and I do find it difficult to accept and somewhat disquieting to even consider"

"I understand your reticence, Abberline, sexual gratification involving regurgitation is hardly commonplace. However, it would explain Chapman's desire to draw out the initialization and continuation of his wives' illnesses over a period of weeks or perhaps months, alternating legitimate treatments with his administrations of poison in order to prolong the demented gratification of his obscene lust."

"My word, Holmes, I have never heard of anything so outlandish in all my days."

"I dare say you have not," Holmes agreed. "This is most certainly a singular case."

"But Holmes, are you equating the actions and preferences of this man with the man who committed the mutilations in Whitechapel and America, if we are still in agreement that they are the same man?

"Certainly, Abberline. It should provide you some satisfaction that your initial theory about Chapman is true. I can assure you, without reservation, that the Whitechapel murderer, Klosowski as we then knew him, and this man Chapman are one in the same."

"But Holmes, is it not true that a long-held axiom in the world of criminal investigation is that perpetrators maintain the same modus operandi throughout their careers? In fact they can be identified by such evidence. I must confess, Holmes, that I have started to doubt as to whether these acts, from Whitechapel to the present time, were committed by the same man."

117

"I agree with you for the most part, Abberline, however there are exceptions to that rule, of which this case is a prime example. We must first understand that women mean nothing to Chapman. His attitude is beyond disdain; it is a dismissal. It is not that he is a misogynist. They simply exist as a means to an end, which is to satisfy an urgency. Above all, he is thoroughly criminally insane, yet his animal cunning is without equal. In this we must recognize that the acts of perversion were merely tools he used to mollify or quench this undefinable, deviant thirst."

"Agreed, Holmes, but how does that explain that this one man can be, if you will excuse the expression, so diverse in his methodology?"

"I can appreciate your hesitancy, Abberline, but please bear with me and try to pay attention as I attempt to make things clear, or as clear as is possible under the circumstances.

"First, Chapman's sadistic sexual urge for blood and mutilation by way of brutal homicide may have been satisfied or had become no longer effective in satisfying that urge. He had to find some other method. On one of his night rambles he may have discovered to his surprise and pleasure that the sight of one of his female companions becoming ill gave him an exhilaration comparable to that he had heretofore experienced only in the commission of atrocities such as those in Whitechapel. So you see, he may have experienced a fortuitous revelation that his urges could be satisfied in a much less flamboyant manner. Thus he might have made a conscious decision that slow poisoning would extend his ecstasy and ultimately prove to be much more satisfying than a violent tete-à-tete, shall we put it, of an evening.

"Secondly, to approach it purely pragmatically, Chapman had been nearly apprehended on a number of occasions both here and in America. He realised that this called for an adjustment such as a change of scenery, which prompted his emigration to America and likewise, after a time, his return to England. Since in both cases he assumed the coast was clear, he had every reason to feel confident.

"Lastly, I have explained that by his assumption of the Chapman surname, he wanted to rid himself of the man Klosowski who had committed the crimes. Yet he could not resist appropriating the name of an early victim as a trophy, particularly since he had appropriated it from the daughter of that victim and then impregnated her. It must have delighted him immensely at the time and may continue to do so to this day.

"So you see, Abberline, Chapman's tastes have been altered not alleviated and his tactics and strategies likewise adapted to this alteration to satisfy his unnatural hunger. In point of fact, there can be little doubt that his tastes were beginning to change with his attempted strangulation of his wife Lucy in New Jersey in 1892."

"My word, Holmes! I believe you've convinced me. But how in creation did you arrive at your conclusions?"

"My methods of deduction in this case consist of an analysis based on the extrapolation of facts combined with the results gained from behavioural and scientific studies peculiar to the situation at hand, to wit the unimaginably abominable activities of a madman."

Part III
Chapter Two

In spite of Holmes's slight trepidation in regard to a premature celebration, it was decided that in light of a fast approaching conclusion to our efforts, a rewarding meal at The Criterion would not be out of order. Following the meal, Abberline continued on to Scotland Yard, where Chief Inspector Godley had invited him to spend the night in order to be close at hand for any eventualities. Holmes insisted that I stay overnight at Baker Street. I would not have had it any other way.

The following morning, we were visited by Abberline who asked if we would accompany him to The Crown to witness the removal of Maud's body to the mortuary, where the post mortem would be conducted. Although our presence would flout protocol, due to the distinctive nature of the case, an exception was made to accommodate us.

Considering the extraordinary progress of events thus far, it came as no surprise to us that when we arrived in Borough High Street, we found The Crown to be open. The main room on the ground floor was doing a brisk business. I could not help but observe to Holmes that in my opinion this was nothing less than as morbid, callous, and ghoulish display of disrespect as ever I had witnessed. Holmes nodded in agreement, but his attention was taken by Chapman who, with his mother-in-law attending his recently deceased wife on the floor above, busily encouraged the goings-on until he caught sight of Abberline. His antics immediately ceased as he made his way over to us. Shoulders stooped and in what he assumed was a contrite manner said, "Hello, Inspector. I expected you would arrive earlier. I know this appears that I am unfeeling, but I assure you I am not. I simply could not grieve any longer. As they say, the best antidote for grief is work, and so life goes on," he continued by indicating round the room.

"Quite," said Abberline as his eyes followed the man's gesture.

"And who are these gentlemen you have brought with you, Inspector? I believe I remember them from yesterday. Surely they are not the undertaker's men?"

"Not in the sense you intend, I am sure," said Abberline. "No. This is Mr. Sherlock Holmes and this is his colleague, Dr. John Watson."

For the briefest moment, apprehension flashed in Chapman's eyes and he drew back perceptively. Recovering, he extended his hand and said, "Well, well, Dr. Watson. Mr. Holmes. I am flattered and I must say a bit surprised that the unfortunate, but ordinary, death of a barmaid would draw the attention of such an esteemed duo."

While I looked down at Chapman's hand, Holmes continued to stare directly into the man's eyes. "Forgive me Mr...Chapman, is it? This is not a social call and for this and other reasons, I prefer not to shake hands."

The arrival of men from the coroner's office precluded any response from Chapman. We accompanied them up the stairs and proceeded to comfort Mrs. Marsh as they secured Maud's body and brought her downstairs to the ambulance for transport to the mortuary in Guy's Hospital.

In order to preclude any further interaction with Chapman at this time, we made straightaway for our waiting cab. Abberline left us at Baker Street, where we had decided it was best that I should remain as Holmes's guest while the drama played itself out. As we waited for the outcome of the post mortem, we spent that Friday conversing about how this singular case had developed, transformed, and in fact mutated over the past fourteen years.

The following morning, we had just finished a light Scottish breakfast of eggs, tattie scone, lorne sausage, and tea that Mrs. Hudson was kind enough to prepare, when Abberline arrived with the results of Maud Marsh's autopsy. Mrs. Hudson passed him on the stairway.

"Inspector," she said, "you're just in time for a spot of tea. I'm sorry but the breakfast has been et."

"Oh, thank you, Mrs. Hudson, but I won't have time for that. Thank you all the same though."

"Abberline," said Holmes, "I trust you have brought us good news, in a manner of speaking."

"Perhaps I have, Holmes, perhaps I have. Dr. James Bodmer was the physician who performed the procedure as witnessed and assisted by Dr. John Stevenson and Dr. Arthur Freiberger."

"Yes, yes, and the results?" asked Holmes.

"Instructed by Dr. Grapel to search for evidence of arsenic poisoning, Dr. Bodmer discovered exactly that."

Holmes leapt up from his chair as if on fire. "What's that you say? Arsenic?"

"Why yes, Holmes, and he informed Coroner Hicks of it straightaway. It was quite enough to open a coroner's court of inquiry and for the police to begin an official investigation."

"Yes, of course, of course it was," said Holmes as he regained his composure. "Now tell me Abberline, would you happen to know which test was used by Dr. Bodmer to determine the poison?"

"Yes, I believe I have it here," Abberline said as he consulted his notebook. "According to Dr. Bodmer, he used the Reinsch test, which is the one commonly employed in an instance such as this."

"Quite right, Abberline. That is the commonly used test for the presence of arsenic. And of course an inquiry and official investigation would be forthcoming. That is proper procedure and it will have to suffice for the present. Watson," he said turning toward me, "make a note that it is imperative that we speak with Coroner Hicks as soon as is feasible. Now then, have you anything more, Abberline?"

"Just this" he answered. "I assume that you would care to accompany me to The Crown, where Chief Inspector Godley and Inspector Neil are awaiting our arrival before they place Mr. Chapman under arrest."

"I can think of nothing Watson and I would enjoy more than to be present at that auspicious occasion."

The date was Saturday, the 25th of October, and we found our trip to The Crown to be slow-going, due to the fact that this was the day of the Royal Progress through South London following the coronation of Edward VII, the previous August. Arriving at our destination at nearly noon, we found that Chapman had adorned The Crown with flags and decorations. In addition, the pub's windows and sidewalk were filled with visitors who had apparently paid for the privilege to watch from such a vantage point as the procession passed.

"How interesting," said Holmes. "Chapman appears to be holding a celebration. One might reasonably ask if it is a celebration for his newly crowned king or his newly deceased wife. Either way, I believe his exhilaration is about to be tempered."

As I contemplated the implications of such a question, I caught the eye of Godley and Neil as they stood against the building to one side of the door. With them were two uniformed constables. After a perfunctory greeting, the constables remaining outside, the inspectors led us into the barroom that teemed with customers. Chapman held forth behind the bar. He did not notice us as with Abberline and Inspector Neil, we stood aside and watched CI Godley make his way toward him.

Approaching the bar, Godley gained Chapman's attention. "You are Mr. Chapman, the publican here?"

"I am that," Chapman said, still unawares.

"I wish to speak with you privately," Godley continued.

"Good god, man! Can you not see how busy I am? Can it not wait?

"I am afraid not. This is quite serious."

With a querulous look, Chapman stared at Godley for a moment and then returned behind the counter, whereupon he left the bar in the care of one of the patrons, who appeared to be familiar with the operation. "All right," he said. "I can spare a few minutes. Come with me into the parlour."

As he made his way toward the back, he finally saw Abberline, Inspector Neil, Holmes and myself. It was then that the penny dropped as he realised the gravity of the situation.

Once in the parlour, Chapman's demeanour changed from curiosity to barely controlled outrage. Before he could vent, the Chief Inspector identified himself. "I am Chief Inspector Godley, inspector for this district. Maud Marsh, who has been living with you as your wife, has been poisoned with arsenic, and in consideration of the surrounding circumstances, I shall take you to the police station while I make inquiries."

Chapman was indignant. "I know nothing about it. I do not know how she got the poison. She has been in Guy's Hospital for sickness. Perhaps there was an accident."

"Hmm. An accident, you say," mused Godley. "I dare say we must look into that, mustn't we? In the meantime, Inspector Neil shall take charge of you to be accompanied by the two constables in order to escort you to headquarters."

Holmes and I proceeded with Abberline and Godley to the bedroom where Maud had died, where we conducted an extensive search. We noted that the bedding and all of Maud's clothing had been removed and no doubt destroyed by Chapman to prevent the discovery of any lingering evidence that might be used against him. For a time we were stymied. Holmes stood motionless in the middle of the room as he studied the positioning of the bed and the several pieces of furniture. Stepping to the closet, he opened the door and examined the closet's depth.

"Something is not quite right here, Watson. Judging by the position of the bed frame against the outer wall of the closet, the interior dimensions of the closet seem to be lacking an unaccounted for two feet in length. Here, come help me shift the bed."

Moving the bed away from the wall revealed a small locked cupboard at floor level. As Holmes made ready to apply his skill with a pen knife to the door of the cupboard, Abberline approached. "Holmes, wait. Do you think that it is possible that Chapman was considerate enough to have included the key to the cupboard among the collection of keys on this ring?"

"My word, Abberline. Where did you find those?"

"I noticed them as we passed by the end of the bar downstairs and thought they might prove to be useful in our search."

"Abberline," said Holmes with a slight laugh, "your talents might well have stood you in good stead on the other side of the law, had you wished to apply them. I am proud of you."

After some false starts, Holmes succeeded in opening the cupboard door. Inside we found a collection of papers, to include bills relating to the funerals of Bessie Taylor and Mary Spink, documents referencing the names Chapman and, interestingly enough Klosowski, as well as a loaded American revolver. While Godley leant over his shoulder, Holmes suddenly stood up, causing Godley to stumble back. "Hello, what have we here, then?" He held up three labelled bottles such as would be obtained from a chemist. The bottles were indeed from a chemist shop: that of W. Davidson of Hastings,

Sussex. Each label also bore the name of its former contents: tartar emetic.

"Holmes," Godley said, "please be more careful. Now, what have you found?"

"Holmes," I asked, "if I may?"

"Be my guest, Watson."

"What we have found here, Chief Inspector, as I am sure Abberline will agree, is the key to Chapman's fate. Though this evidence is circumstantial, it does not mean that it is inaccurate. Convictions have been attained in the past on the strength of strong circumstantial evidence, as you are aware. These prescription labels from chemist's bottles are Chapman's souvenirs – game trophies, if you will, reminiscent of how the Ripper retained pieces of his victim's organs or clothing. When coupled with testimony and ancillary evidence, these labels should be more than enough to ensure that our Mr. Chapman becomes intimately acquainted with British justice."

"Well put, Watson. I could not improve on that analysis myself," said Holmes. "And now I should think it would be a capital idea if we conveyed the fruits of our labours to the authorities. Abberline: would you be so kind as to provide us transport?"

"It would be more than my pleasure."

Part III
Chapter Three

Chief Inspector Godley took his leave of us at Scotland Yard, while we proceeded on to The Old Bailey, where we sought an interview with the district coroner, Mr. Athelstan Braxton Hicks. No sooner had we been announced when we were admitted to Mr. Hicks's office. The gentleman stood and crossed from behind his desk to greet us.

"Mr. Holmes, Dr. Watson, your reputations precede you." Shaking hands all round, he continued, "Abberline, Chief Inspector Godley has informed me that you are responsible for introducing Holmes and Watson to this matter."

"That I am, Mr. Hicks and with their help and advice, we may at last bring to a conclusion all matters concerning Mr. Chapman."

"I see," said Hicks as he returned behind his desk and gestured to several chairs. "Please seat yourselves and tell me what you have discovered."

"Thank you for seeing us, Mr. Hicks," said Holmes. "It is my understanding that Dr. Bodmer has completed his post-mortem of Maud Marsh and that he found sufficient amounts of arsenic in her system to warrant the detention of Mr. Chapman while inquiries are being made."

"That is correct, Mr. Holmes."

"If you will excuse my presumptuousness, sir, but it is my considered opinion that you should advise Chief Inspector Godley to proceed forthwith to arrest Mr. Chapman on the charge of murder, so that he might be held – and again in my opinion – without bail until a full investigation can be completed."

"I see. What reason do you have to make such a suggestion, if I may ask?"

"To begin at the beginning then, with Abberline's help, Watson and I have discovered compelling pieces of evidence from Mr. Chapman's residence that tend to confirm our suspicions as to the murder of Maud Marsh and the true nature of our Mr. George Chapman."

"Please, go on."

"Secured within a hidden cupboard were a number of medicine bottles such as those one would obtain from a chemist. The labels on the bottles indicated that they had been obtained from William Davidson, a chemist practising in Hastings. The labels also indicated that they had previously contained tartar emetic, which is the popular name for antimony potassium tartrate. Antimony is extremely dangerous when ingested, and can elicit symptoms similar to those of arsenic poisoning, and can very easily lead to death. Incidentally, it is also considerably more lethal than arsenic."

"But Mr. Holmes, Dr. Bodmer's post mortem did not yield any evidence of antimony."

""That is not surprising, Mr. Hicks. The procedure which Dr. Bodmer ran, the Reinsch Test, is generally used to detect only arsenic"

"What do you recommend, Mr. Holmes?"

"First, I recommend another test and that the more invasive procedure of an autopsy be performed. Secondly, I suggest that someone other than Dr. Bodmer conduct the procedure. Watson has informed me that Dr. Stevenson and Dr. Freiberger, who assisted Dr. Bodmer, have stellar qualifications and would not be tainted by previous results or instructions. Third, I suggest that they be directed to conduct the Marsh Test, which not only detects the presence of arsenic but also that of mercury and antimony.

"Incidentally, Watson and I visited the chemist shop of William Davidson, who readily admitted to having sold tartar emetic to Mr. Chapman on a number of occasions since 1897 and in compliance with the law, has records to that effect."

"I must say Holmes, in addition to further inquiries, this evidence is certainly compelling enough for me to call for an autopsy and test and to remand Mr. Chapman on a charge of murder."

"I have one more piece of information that, unless I am in error which is unlikely, will shed considerable light on certain activities that took place in Whitechapel fourteen years ago."

"What do you mean?"

"Among the dividends we salvaged from the cupboard were a collection of documents that gave clear indication that George Chapman was in fact one Severin Klosowski who, as you might recall, was an individual of prime interest during the reign of terror instituted by the so-called Jack the Ripper. I must tell you that Abberline discovered years ago the singular fact that Severin Klosowski had disappeared into the persona of George Chapman under what can only be termed questionable circumstances. These papers only attest to that fact. In light of the man's proclivity to change identities as well as locations, I can only emphasise to you that there is a distinct possibility, dare I say probability, that he would take any opportunity to escape and therefore should be held without bail."

"My word, Mr. Holmes, we must not let this man out of our custody! I shall instruct Inspector Godley to call on our Mr. Chapman in his present quarters at Newgate and invite him to remain with us for the foreseeable future."

"Mr. Hicks," Holmes interjected, "we would be honoured if you would allow us to convey your wishes to CI Godley. Also, while I realise that this request might be out of order, would it be possible for Abberline, Watson and myself to accompany the chief inspector when he delivers the news to Mr. Chapman?"

"Mr. Holmes," said Coroner Hicks as he rose from behind his desk, "in my opinion, your contributions to this case have been of inestimable value. Since I have jurisdiction in this matter, I see no reason why you may not be allowed to assist Chief Inspector Godley on his mission."

We expressed our thanks and exited the office. Locating Godley at his office, we conveyed the news and made ready to make the journey next door to the venerable Newgate Prison.

Godley conducted us in, through the receiving room, through another door, and along a rather dank corridor to what might be termed a holding or temporary cell, where we found Chapman, alone, seated at a table. Considering the circumstances in which he found himself, the prisoner seemed reasonably calm: annoyed rather than angry. As the door was unlocked and we entered the cell, Chapman stood, an expectant look on his face. Godley stepped toward him.

"Chief Inspector, I see you have come to arrange bail for me."

"That is not my intention at this time, Mr. Chapman. In light of certain evidence obtained from your rooms, it is my duty to charge you with the willful murder of Maud Marsh by poisoning her with arsenic."

"But I am innocent. Can I not have bail?"

"No sir, you may not. Presently, you are to appear before a magistrate to be remanded in custody until such a time as you will be formally arraigned, charged, and brought to trial."

Chapman looked rapidly between Holmes, Abberline and myself before focusing once more on Godley. "But I am innocent, I tell you."

"That is yet to be determined," said Godley as we all turned to leave.

When we had exited the hallway and re-entered the receiving room, Holmes stopped and turned to Godley. "I wonder, Chief Inspector, if I might try your patience and ask you to turn a blind eye to procedure once again?"

"What do you have in mind?"

"I should like to have a private audience with the prisoner."

"I see," said Godley, with just the slightest trace of indignation. "It is a considerable departure from regulations, and by all rights I am obligated to deny such a request."

"Indeed you are, Chief Inspector. I understand your obligation and I fully accept the possibility of your adherence to it. However, I am quite certain that by way of a private interview, I will be able to shed more light on the question of motivation, which could go a considerable way toward a swift conviction. Of course, I would expect my colleague, Dr. Watson, to be in attendance in order to lend his considerable insightful analytical talents to the process and to act as a recorder of the conversation."

Godley looked to Abberline, "Well Abberline, what is your opinion in regard to this matter?"

"I have no official standing …"

"I am well aware of that, but your experience in the case is without equal. Insofar as I am concerned, that grants you standing, official or otherwise."

"In that case, it is my considered opinion that you could not do better, and you could do far worse, than to allow Holmes and Watson access to our friend."

"Very well then," said Godley, as he handed me the key to the holding cell. "Mr. Holmes, Dr. Watson, you may have at him. Abberline and I shall wait in the receiving room."

Part III
Chapter Four

With that understanding, we strode back down the hallway and approached the holding cell. Chapman was standing at the door with a look of anticipation that only increased the closer we came to him.

"Please step back, sir," I instructed as I unlocked the cell door.

"Oh, I am indeed glad you came back, Mr. Holmes, Dr. Watson. You are fair men, I know and will be able to see the injustice I am being made to suffer."

Holmes gave a short start and the smallest of laughs. "Well sir, I am certain you are intimately familiar with both injustice and suffering. My only confusion here is the question of injustice and suffering on the part of whom. But we will address that momentarily. For the moment, it would satisfy me if you would identify yourself."

"What do you mean?" said Chapman. "I am George Chapman."

"No sir, you may call yourself George Chapman, but there was no George Chapman prior to 1894."

"Yes sir, I am George Chapman and I am from America."

"You are an American?"

"Yes, I was born in New Jersey."

"Hmm," said Holmes, "I must say that though you speak English very well, I do detect an accent."

"Yes, of course."

"It is not an American accent, of which there are many. No sir, yours is a Polish accent, from the Warsaw area if I am not mistaken, and of course I am not."

"You are correct, Mr. Holmes. You have an excellent ear. I can explain. I was orphaned at an early age in America and was raised by foster parents in Warsaw, who saw to my upbringing and training."

"Ah yes, your training. Would it surprise you that I discovered certain papers that had been concealed in a cupboard in your rooms above The Crown that attest to attendance and training in practical surgery at the Praga Hospital in Warsaw in 1885 and 1886?"

"Yes, yes, I received training there but returned to America, where I was only able to find employment as a barber's assistant. Finally, I came to England for the first time in 1893 and worked as a barber's assistant."

"I see. Would it further surprise you that among the papers I found were certain documents attesting to the birth, origin, occupation, and knowledge of various drugs under the name of Severin Klosowski?"

"I do not know this fellow. Who is he?"

"It is my contention, Mr. Chapman, and the contention of my colleague Dr. Watson, as well as that of the authorities, that he is in fact you."

"No, I do not know anything about him."

"That is indeed fascinating, Mr. Klosowski…"

"No! Do not call me by that name! That is not me!"

"Very well, Mr. Chapman, very well. But you see, Mr. Klosowski ceased to exist the moment you came into existence. Does not that singular occurrence strike you as odd?"

"No, it does not and what does it have to do with me?"

"It may well have everything to do with you, Mr. Chapman. For you see in London in 1889, this man Klosowski was married — and is still officially married — to a woman named Lucy Baderski. In 1892, that unsatisfactory union ended while the couple resided in New Jersey and Klosowski tried to murder her."

"I do not know what…"

"Shortly thereafter, Lucy returned to England. Klosowski followed and attempted to reconnect with her, but she would have none of it. Klosowski deserted her and her newborn child and disappeared for a time. You, excuse me, he surfaced as an assistant at another hairdressing establishment whereupon he met a woman named Annie Georgina Chapman, whom he later took as a common law wife. Does this not sound at all familiar to you, Mr. Klosowski?"

"No it does not and I insist you not call me by that name, damn you!"

"Oh yes, that's right, I apologise. That will change presently. Klosowski soon tired of this relationship and it too ended. It is at this point where the plot thickens. Klosowski did take something from this so-called marriage: he more or less appropriated the name of his common law wife and became George Chapman, that is to say Klosowski became you."

"Damn you to hell!" Chapman yelled and lunged at Holmes. Before I could react, Holmes, with a neat, clean, and quick application of the baritsu technique that had spelled the demise of Professor Moriarty so many years ago, had Chapman gasping for breath on the floor of his cell.

"Allow me to continue," Holmes said to the supine figure before us. "I find it more than interesting that this woman, Annie Georgina Chapman, was the daughter of one Annie Chapman, who was the second victim of the monster called Jack the Ripper."

"I know nothing of this," gasped Chapman as he dragged himself up to be seated at the table.

"No, of course you don't," said Holmes as he crossed the cell to a point behind Chapman. "That atrocity took place in 1888 and you were in America at the time, weren't you?"

"No, I mean yes. You are trying to confuse me – just as you confuse me with this Klosowski fellow. I don't know him, I tell you."

"Yes, quite," said Holmes. "You wouldn't want to be confused with Klosowski, would you? He was one of the main suspects at the time of the Ripper murders and still is, I dare say. You see, he has disappeared and remains at large."

"Then why are you bothering with me? I am innocent of these crimes. You should be chasing him."

Holmes looked up at me. "As far as I can tell, Mr. Chapman, you have not been accused of the Ripper murders. Why are you pleading innocence?"

"I know of these murders, of course. You cannot trick me. I heard of them in America. They had nothing to do with me." He paused for a moment at this point and then looked directly at me. "They were cheap women anyway who were nothing. They made no difference to me or to anyone else. Rubbish. You understand, don't you, Doctor?"

I had no response to that question.

"Maybe this Klosowski – is that his name? Maybe he did the world a favour. These cheap whores spread disease and hate men really. I know. I have been around them." He then shook his head and gave a short, "Ha."

Holmes and I again exchanged silent looks. This seemed to be as close to a confirmed confession as we were likely to obtain at this point. It certainly would serve as a point of departure for interrogation by King's Counsel, if Chapman were to be brought to trial for the Ripper murders.

"I think," said Holmes, "that perhaps we might dispense with this topic of conversation for the time being, don't you?"

"Yes, I do. It is useless, a waste of time. All I know of this Klosowski is what you have just told me. I would just as soon leave him behind."

"I'm sure you would," said Holmes. "We can always return to him later. Now, let me ask you about Maud: Why did you kill her?"

Chapman started to rise in protest, but one look from Holmes and he resumed his seat. "I do not know why you say I killed her nor why I am being held in this matter."

"I believe that Chief Inspector Godley has explained to you that you are being held because Maud, that is your common law wife, has been determined to have been killed by arsenic poisoning and that you are a suspect."

"Yes, Mr. Holmes, I understand that I am being accused, but it is not true."

"I tend to agree with you, Mr. Chapman."

"Oh thank you, Mr. Holmes! I knew you would be fair with me."

"I believe, Mr. Chapman, that Maud was not a victim of arsenic poisoning, but that she was the victim of antimony poisoning and that she was poisoned by you."

"How dare you say that Mr. Holmes? I would not have hurt her for the world. She had wanted to have a baby with me, when she was took ill. I would not have hurt her for anything."

"I will admit that your sincerity is impressive, but it flies in the face of fact."

"Mr. Holmes," said Chapman in an almost collegial manner, "you are intelligent and you have had experience with murders of all types. True?"

"True."

"Then surely you realise that if my poor Maud had been poisoned, it would have killed her quickly, almost immediately."

"Yes, that is true, Mr. Chapman and that is one of the mistakes you made."

"What do you mean?"

"What I mean, Mr. Chapman, is that Dr. Grapel was perfectly correct when he discerned that Maud was in the process of being slowly poisoned. He conveyed that belief to Mrs. Marsh. It was at this point that sometime during the last evening of Maud's life, you were overcome with panic – doctors and investigators were getting too close. In order to be rid of the threat, you administered a large, fatal dose of antimony potassium tartrate, thus ensuring an end to the tragedy. This was the selfsame toxin you had been administering to her intermittently for some time – alternating the dosages with legitimate medicines that had been prescribed by doctors. I have made a deductive study of you, Mr. Chapman, which study has led me to the realization that the torture you inflicted on poor Maud was nothing less than the satisfaction of a sadistic, sexual lust that in itself was the exhibition of ultimate control."

Chapman gripped the table and shook with anger as once again he began to rise. By this point I had crossed behind him and as he rose, I firmly grasped his shoulders and thrust him back into his chair.

"Further," Holmes continued, "you assumed that Maud's death would be misdiagnosed as her having succumbed to severe gastroenteritis, or some such. Grapnel's only error was attributing Maud's death to arsenic poisoning. Your error was in believing in the diagnosis and that it would not be investigated with an eye toward anything other than arsenic poisoning, and that the results would, at best, be inconclusive."

Chapman appeared to regain some control of himself. "I did not poison my wife, I tell you! I did not! You must believe me! I implore you!"

At this point, I could not help but intercede. I moved around the table so that I might face him. "Mr. Chapman. Not only do we believe that you poisoned your most recent wife, but we also believe that you poisoned two of your previous wives as well."

"No!"

"I am afraid," said Holmes in a conciliatory fashion, "that Dr. Watson's statement is quite accurate and that you have inadvertently provided the evidence which tends to support the claim."

"What do you mean?"

"I mean that among your cache of items – souvenirs if you will – I discovered in your secret cupboard were three empty medicine bottles, such as you might obtain from a chemist – indeed which you did obtain from a chemist: Mr. William Davidson of High Street in Hastings, according to the information on the labels. The labels also made note that the bottles had contained antimony potassium tartrate. Do you have any explanation to offer?"

Chapman's dark eyes narrowed and flitted from side to side, giving the impression of a trapped animal. "I have none. Those things are not mine."

"Really, Mr. Chapman," I said, "they were found in your rooms, in your cupboard along with other effects..."

Chapman leapt to his feet, "Yes, that is right!" he cried. "Other effects, papers with the name of that man Klosowski on them! It was him! He must have been the one who bought the poison! Don't you see?"

Holmes shook his head, "Mr. Chapman, I applaud you for your truthfulness. Thank you. What's more, I agree with you; Klosowski was the man who purchased the poison."

Chapman let out a heavy sigh, laughed and sat back down as a smile beamed forth from under his heavy moustache.

Smiling his thin smile, Holmes turned to me. "Come, Watson, I believe we should convey the good news to Abberline and Chief Inspector Godley."

Chapman stood back up as we exited the cell and locked it behind us. "Yes," he said, "you tell them that. If poor Maud was poisoned, it was that man Klosowski who did it. Tell them I must have bail. I have a business to run, after all"

"Ah yes, bail," said Holmes. "I'm afraid that would be quite impossible."

"But why?"

"You see, Mr. Chapman. You have just suggested that it must have been Klosowski who purchased the tartar-emetic from Mr. Davidson's chemist shop in Hastings."

"Yes, yes. Go on."

"I am so sorry, Mr. Chapman, but I neglected to mention that Dr. Watson and I interviewed Mr. Davidson. He informed us that dating back to 1897, he had sold a number of bottles of tartar-emetic to a certain individual. As required by law, he recorded the sales and the name of the purchaser in his ledger. We were shown the ledger, by Mr. Davidson. The name of the purchaser was recorded as Mr. George Chapman. Unless I am incorrect, which is highly unlikely, Mr. Davidson will appear at your forthcoming trial and bring his ledger, which King's Counsel will undoubtedly present as evidence. So you see Mr. Chapman, by your suggestion that Klosowski made the purchases, you have de facto admitted that you and Klosowski are one and the same."

Chapman gripped the bars and shook them with a ferocity that I feared would rip the door from its hinges, "No!" he cried, "You have tricked me! I did not say that! I am not Klosowski! You cannot tell them that I am! I do not know him. I... I..."

"Yes, Mr. Chapman. Thank you again for your cooperation. I am certain that we shall see you again." With that farewell and Chapman's voice echoing off the walls of the corridor, Holmes and I passed through the outer door and into the receiving area where Godley and Abberline awaited us.

We explained the results of our interview to Godley and Abberline. Abberline was particularly excited about Chapman's tacit admission to being Klosowski. Clapping Godley on the back he exclaimed, "There it is, Godley! You've got Jack the Ripper at last!"

"My dear Abberline," said Holmes, "although you may be correct – and I honestly believe that you are, I would advise against another early celebration of victory. In the absence of empirical evidence and the passage of so many years, the establishment of Chapman as Jack the Ripper is far from a certainty. As you are aware, the soundness of testimony of eyewitnesses as to the identification of suspects, never reliable and often contradictory to begin with, only erodes with the passage of time. I am afraid that in lieu of a full confession on Chapman's part that he is Klosowski and that he committed the Ripper murders, the chances of a conviction in that matter are minimal. Believe me when I tell you that I tried to impress on Chapman that I was his last best hope for the redemption of his very soul by his admission to being Klosowski. Such an appeal was wasted. He appears adamant in his conviction that not only is he not Klosowski, but that he is completely unfamiliar with, as he put it, that man.

"By way of the evidence we have compiled in regard to his brutish behaviour toward his wives, for want of a better term, and his similar behaviour toward his female companions on his late night interactions with them, as well as his expression that the Ripper may have been performing a service, it is quite clear that Chapman is a misogynist of the first order.

"However, I must refer you to the theory put forth by Dr. Pierre Jenet and Dr. Sigmund Freud. It seems that Mr. Chapman may be a perfect example of a dissociative identity, in which the individual automatically dissociates himself from unacceptable thoughts and or, in this case, actions. In this, it is a distinct possibility that when Chapman claims not to be Klosowski, he is stating his firm belief; he has dissociated himself from that part of himself. I would be very surprised if he ever acknowledges that he is Klosowski and in that, Jack the Ripper.

"In regard to the other aspect of this case, when the results of Maud's autopsy are made known, I am certain that we shall find that she was the victim of antimony poisoning and that circumstances will dictate that it could only have been Chapman who administered the poison."

We agreed to part while we waited for the results of the autopsy. We did not have long to wait. For convenience, I had remained at Baker Street with Holmes. We spent the following two days deep in discussion as to all the events which had led us up to this point. Of course I took copious notes, so as not to leave a single detail unmined or delineated less than perfectly. On the afternoon of the third day, Abberline and Godley arrived at our door. The autopsy results had come in and were ready for our perusal at the offices of Coroner Hicks.

Arriving at the Old Bailey, we made our way to Hicks's anteroom, whereupon we were immediately ushered into the coroner's office. Hicks could barely contain himself as, brandishing a sheaf of papers, he rose and crossed the floor to greet us. "Gentlemen," he fairly shouted, "I have received the results of the autopsy and they are just as you predicted! As you suggested, Dr. Stevenson and Dr. Freiberger performed the Marsh test and discovered that the poor woman had enough antimony in her body to have killed a great many people. Antimony poisoning was indeed the cause of her death. Congratulations."

"I hardly think that congratulations are called for," said Holmes, "in light of the circumstances."

"Yes of course," Hicks said sheepishly. "I only meant that your investigation and recommendations have combined to render a favourable outcome so that a successful prosecution of Mr. Chapman will surely follow."

"In that case," said Holmes, "on behalf of Dr. Watson and our two colleagues, I accept your congratulations and I hope that you will be open enough to accept one further recommendation from me."

"Please continue," said Coroner Hicks, "I am listening."

"In an issue of the *London Daily Post,* at the time of the Ripper slayings, Inspector Frederick Abberline put forth the theory that this series of horrible events in Whitechapel were perpetrated by a single individual. As I mentioned to you in our earlier conversation, it is our contention that the Whitechapel Ripper and George Chapman are the same person."

"Yes, I remember. Go on."

"Based on my own practical study and research into the matter, the murderous habits of a sequential killer are what one might consider to be an addiction, which may be caused by any number of factors, internal and external. By the very nature of addictions, the habits will continue ad infinitum until brought to a halt by an external factor."

"Yes?"

"In the case of Mr. Chapman, it is my belief that he is the Whitechapel murderer and that the cessation of his activities was only a temporary respite. His blood lust did not end but rather transmogrified. This transmogrification may have been brought on by a transitory satiation of his urge or desire or by way of a conscious decision on his part, having sensed that apprehension was threatening. As a consequence, if he were still to be able to satisfy his needs, his methodology had to change. Through Abberline's connections in America, we were able to pinpoint when that change took place. After he had committed several Ripper-like murders in America, he was foiled by chance in his attempt to murder his wife and confessed to her that it had been his intent to virtually butcher her."

"My word, Mr. Holmes!"

"She escaped and successfully fled to England, but Chapman – at that time still Klosowski – sensed that the authorities were closing in on him and so he also returned to England. Though he relocated to the Whitechapel district with his unnatural desires unabated, it was then that his methods changed from outright mutilation to the less-detectable mechanism of poison. His lustful urges transformed from short-term, brutal and bloody sadism to the more insidious technique of long, drawn-out physical pain and suffering, which he could control and enjoy until he put an end to it."

"I must confess, Mr. Holmes, that is the most remarkable analysis I have ever heard! What are your suggestions?"

"To begin with, as we have discovered through our interview with Mr. Chapman, he will not or perhaps cannot confess to the Whitechapel murders. He not only denies having committed the murders, he denies being or even having heard of Severin Klosowski. Because of the passage of time since those murders, proof of his guilt beyond a reasonable doubt would be impossible to establish. What we are left to deal with are the murders of Maud Marsh, Bessie Taylor and Mary Spink.

"Through your good offices, we have established that Maud was a victim of antimony poisoning. I am quite certain that testimony by her parents, family members and outside individuals will demonstrate that Chapman was the only person who could have administered the poison to the poor girl.

"It is my suggestion that orders for the exhumation of the bodies of Bessie Taylor and Mary Spink be issued with the declared intent being to perform autopsies in order to determine the true cause of death of each of them."

"I understand, Mr. Holmes, but if I am not in error…" At this, Mr. Hicks returned to his desk and shuffled through several documents. "Yes, here it is. The causes of death were determined shortly following the demise of each woman. They were gastroenteritis in the case of Mary Spink in 1897 and intestinal obstruction in the case of Bessie Taylor in 1901. That the causes of death have been established and recorded would necessarily preclude anyone from disturbing the corpses further, which of course would include the act of exhumation and certainly that of an autopsy."

Holmes paused momentarily, silently nodded and then said, "Of course I can appreciate what you are saying, Mr. Hicks; however, I believe that the evidence we have collected and presented to you and the authorities speaks to special, extenuating circumstances. To put it to you in a straightforward manner; for want of propriety, a sequential murderer may go unpunished and the deaths of innocent young women go unavenged."

"Well, Mr. Holmes, you certainly have a most emphatic and cogent manner of putting things. I will take your suggestion under consideration but you must realise that this would call for the convening of a Coroner's Court."

"I do understand that, Mr. Hicks and I further understand that such a process is not immediate and may take some time. In light of this I do implore you, sir, to initiate the process with dispatch. It is also my recommendation that Doctors Stevenson and Feiberger carry out the procedures."

Laying the documents back on his desk, the coroner approached us with his hand extended. "I shall certainly take your recommendation and your reasoning under serious advisement."

As hands were shaken all round, Holmes could not resist one parting shot. "Thank you for your time, Mr. Hicks. If I might make a prediction?"

"Sir?"

"My prediction is twofold. Due to the fact that you are an intelligent man, one dedicated to the proper carriage of justice, you will indeed see to it that the requisite autopsies will be performed. Secondly, I predict that the results of these procedures will number amongst the most clear-cut ever performed by this office."

"You have piqued my interest, Mr. Holmes, indeed you have," Hicks said as he ushered us out of the office.

Abberline and Godley were nearly obsequious as they pleaded for Holmes to decipher and explain his predictions, but to no avail. "Gentlemen, I will only tell you this much. I was quite certain that Mr. Hicks would agree to the autopsies when I appealed to his vanity and sense of justice. That agreement was virtually guaranteed when I asserted that the procedures would be singular in their revelations."

"Yes, yes, Holmes," said Abberline, as Godley looked on expectantly, "just what are these revelations and how did you arrive at them?"

"Ah, gentlemen, revelations are termed such because they are in fact suddenly revealed. Far be it from me to reveal the secrets before their time and spoil the pleasure of your own prognostication and anticipation."

"But Holmes!"

"No gentlemen, my mind is made up. I shall not rob you of your satisfaction when, in due time, you learn of the outcome of the autopsies."

Hands were shaken once again as we went our separate ways: Abberline and Godley to Scotland Yard, Holmes and myself to Baker Street to await further developments.

Part III
Chapter Six

Through the month of November and into December, the Coroner's Court sat four times to hear evidence about the deaths of Maud Marsh, Bessie Taylor and Mary Spink. Chapman remained in custody all of that time. Toward the end of November, we were summoned to the Old Bailey and the office of the coroner.

We arrived at the office to be greeted by Abberline and Godley, who had apparently received similar summonses. Mr. Hicks saw us in and circled back behind his desk. Smiling and shaking his head he said, "Holmes your predictions were absolutely spot on. I was able to circumvent propriety and succeeded in having autopsies authorised to be performed on Taylor and Spink, a fact which you are probably aware of by now. You were also correct in your prediction that the revelations these procedures produced were indeed singular, as you put it. Doctors Stevenson and Freiberger were nonplussed. Stevenson allowed that the condition of the corpses – one more than a year old and the other five years old, was such that they appeared to have been buried nearly as recently as that of Maud Marsh! In addition, there was absolutely no odour of putrefaction."

At this announcement, Abberline and Godley were speechless.

"Yes," said Holmes, "that is exactly the revelation to which I referred. I am certain that either Stevenson or

Freiberger offered you the explanation as to why the bodies were in this unexpected condition."

"They did indeed and they also said that because of this, neither had ever performed such uncomplicated, clear-cut if you will, autopsies."

"That is all very well," said Abberline, "now will you please share your secret with us?"

"Holmes," I asked, "may I?"

"Certainly, Watson. Be my guest."

"Gentlemen, you might assume that a body disinterred after a length of time such as five years would evidence considerable decomposition, would you not?"

"Unquestionably," said Godley.

"Under normal circumstances, that would be the case," I continued. "But these circumstances, as we all agree, are hardly normal. You see, these women died from being poisoned by antimony administered in unusually large amounts. This factor increased the rate of dehydration and retarded the rate of decomposition to the point that the body and the organs all appeared viable and unchanged from as they were at the end of life. This in turn, made it all that much easier to determine and detect the poison itself as well as its disposition throughout the body."

"This is all quite remarkable," said Abberline, "but the prime factor should be that justice will be served and that the Whitechapel fiend will finally receive his due punishment."

"I am sorry, Abberline, as I know how much you would like that statement to be shouted from the rooftops and the victory of your dogged pursuit of the monster officially recognized. Though I do agree with your contention, as I have previously told you, you will have to be satisfied that there is simply no evidence that can be applied to support that conclusion. At this point, anything short of a full confession would preclude any prosecution of Mr. Chapman in regard to the Ripper murders.

"However, you will have the satisfaction of having avenged the murder of three innocent women and in the process, as far as we are concerned, of having vanquished Jack the Ripper."

Three weeks went by until the 18th of December when the final coroner's jury returned a verdict of death by willful murder against George Chapman. On the 31st of December, under the name of Severin Klosowski – to which he vehemently objected – the man was also charged with the willful murders of Mary Spink and Bessie Taylor. He was committed to trial at the Central Criminal Court. It would be almost another three months before the trial actually commenced.

Part Three
Chapter Seven

It was in January of 1903 that my wife's patience with me and my devotion to Sherlock Holmes had begun to erode. Although she was too understanding to issue an ultimatum, it was evident to me that she had begun to feel somewhat neglected. Early in the month, as Holmes put it, I deserted him for a wife. He was left on his own to undertake a case later referred to as "The Adventure of the Blanched Soldier," in an account penned by Holmes himself. This was the first of only two accounts in which I played no part in reportage — other than to suggest that he try writing them himself.

Holmes and I had very little contact until the 16th of March, when the trial finally got under way in Courtroom Number One in the Old Bailey. Godley had interceded on behalf of Abberline, Holmes and myself to ensure that we were afforded seats in the courtroom. Because of the rash of publicity over the previous two months about the upcoming trial of the Borough Poisoner – as the prisoner was now referred to in the press, attendance to the proceedings was in great demand to the point where between civilians and reporters, even standing room was at a premium. Taking into consideration the crowd outside the courtroom, many of whom had brought food and drink, the atmosphere was one of a festival. The possibility that the Borough Poisoner might also be proven to be the fiend Jack the Ripper fueled the intensity and blood lust of the attendees, particularly those in the street.

Presenting the case for the Crown were the Solicitor-General: Mr. Edward Carson, Sir Archibald Bodkin, and Mr. Charles Matthews. Mr. George Elliott, Mr. Vincent Lyons, and Mr. Arthur Hutton appeared for the defence. That one of the most popular judges in Britain, Judge Justice William Grantham, presided over the trial was indicative of the importance of the proceedings.

It is also interesting to note that amongst the spectators were not only members of Maud Marsh's family but also Chapman's legal wife, Lucy Baderski; as well as her sister, Alice; and Alice's husband, Stanislas Rauch.

The gallery virtually erupted with jeers and threats until quieted by the under-sheriff, as directed by Judge Justice Grantham. As the clerk of arraigns was about to read the charges, Holmes nudged me. "Pay attention to this exchange, Watson. It should set the tone for the entire trial."

The clerk read that Severin Klosowski was charged with the willful murders of Mary Spink, Bessie Taylor and Maud Marsh. Chapman stood mute. He was instructed to plead guilty or not guilty. Chapman stared malevolently at his questioner and stated in full voice, "I do not know that name. I do not know that man." The clerk of arraigns looked toward Judge Justice Grantham, who nodded his head in the direction of the prisoner. The clerk of arraigns again asked for a plea, only this time he did not address the prisoner by name. In a low voice, Chapman pleaded not guilty to each charge.

"You see there, Watson, what has happened? The door has been opened to the possibility of Chapman and Klosowski being the same individual. As you know, the Crown has considerable evidence to support that claim which, no doubt, will be presented to confirm the fact in the mind of the jury. That will be the only thing that could serve to link Chapman to the Jack the Ripper slayings. We also know that without a confession and because of contradictory and uncertain witness testimony, I trust that the connection will not be made and he will neither be accused nor convicted of the Ripper slayings, which we are certain he did commit.

"However, now that the judge has allowed this testimony and charges to be admitted, it will undoubtedly influence the jury's eventual deliberation in favour of the Crown."

"Holmes, that sounds to me as if you believe that the verdict is a forgone conclusion."

"And so it is, Watson, and so it is. And in this, justice will be served."

The trial went just as Holmes had predicted. The first day was used largely to emphasise the Klosowski/Chapman connection. Annie Georgina Chapman testified that she had lived with the defendant, who went by the name of Severin Klosowski, and that he had fathered a child with her. She stated that he never used the name of Chapman while he was with her and further that he refused to have anything to do with the baby. To all who were present, this information stood in testament to the nature of Chapman's character.

The details of the murders of Taylor and Spink were exposed at some length. Testimony of witnesses established the fact that it could only have been Klosowski/Chapman who administered the tartar emetic to the victims. Mr. William

Davidson, the chemist from Hastings, gave testimony and offered his ledger, which established the fact that he had provided the tartar emetic to the accused on several occasions. The second day was devoted almost entirely to the murder of Maud Marsh. Witnesses were more plentiful and their testimony more certain and unassailable due to the relative immediacy of the event. Dr. Stevenson, who had performed the second autopsies in all three cases testified that all three women had died from antimony poisoning.

Through all this, attorneys for the accused offered little to no defence in the way of effective cross-examination. It seemed to me that for all intents and purposes, the trial was over. Holmes quickly disabused me of that opinion. "Wait," he said, "the defence has yet to call their witness."

"But who might they call to defend a man whom, I dare say, all here consider to be guilty?

"Watson, I am surprised at you, having reached a conclusion before all evidence has been examined."

"What do you mean, Holmes? There has been overwhelming evidence offered."

"Quite right, my dear fellow, but if I were to hazard a guess, which, as you know, is something I never do, the defence has but one witness it may call."

"Surely you don't mean..." Before I could finish my question and Holmes could answer, Mr. Elliott called George Chapman to the stand. Mr. Elliott proceeded to elicit testimony to the effect that George Chapman had been born in America, orphaned at an early age, worked as a hairdresser, came to England in 1893, and had been terribly unlucky in love, having had a number of wives who died prematurely. He finally attested that he had loved them all dearly, he was being unjustly accused, and he had no idea who could have poisoned them — if indeed they had been poisoned.

Judge Justice Grantham then called Mr. Carson to cross-examine. Holmes was fairly bristling with anticipation as he gave me another nudge. "Now mind this Watson. I have seen the work of the eminent Mr. Carson before. He is brilliantly ruthless when he spots a chink in the armour of an adversary and there is a very large chink indeed in Mr. Chapman's armour.

Of course I was intrigued by what might lay in store and I was not disappointed when the following exchange took place:

"Your real name is Severin Klosowski, is it not?"

"I do not know anything about that other name. Who is that other fellow?"

"That is you – we call you Klosowski."

"I am George Chapman. I have informed the American Consul in London that I am George Chapman from America. I am an American citizen!

"How do you account for the documents found in your home referencing one Severin Klosowski?

"I do not account for them. I do not know about them. I have not been there long. The police must have placed them there. You know how these people hate foreigners."

The cross examination continued in this vein, with both parties occasionally raising their voices: Carson in his interrogation and Klosowski/Chapman in his defiant denials.

The duel in this fashion went on unhindered, as it were, by judicial propriety until the point where Mr. Carson broached the topic of the legal marriage of the accused.

"Are you aware that Lucy Klosowski, who is in this courtroom today and has identified you as her husband, has stated that you did indeed arrive in New York City from England in 1891, and that you threatened her with a large knife after moving to New Jersey?"

"I do not know this woman," he replied. "Who is she?"

The remark had scarcely left his mouth when Lucy leapt up from her seat in the gallery. "Oh Severin, don't say that," she yelled. "You remember the time you nearly killed me in Jersey City!"

The defendant was accusatory as he rose over the railing and addressed the court, "I do not know this woman! Who is she?"

Lucy had to be restrained by her brother-in-law as the gallery once again erupted in calls and threats. Order was restored as Lucy and her family were removed from the courtroom, and Judge Justice Grantham instructed Mr. Carson to continue. The rest of the examination proceeded as Mr. Carson frequently referred to Chapman as Klosowski and Mr. Chapman repeatedly and heatedly rejected the name. Mr. Carson made passing references to the Ripper murders, which visibly rankled the accused and to which the defence objected. The objections were sustained for the reason that they had no relevance to the trial. I mentioned as much to Holmes.

"Of course there's no relevance, my dear fellow, but that is a prosecutorial tactic employed purely for the benefit of the jury. Once something is heard, it cannot be unheard, and the connection is fixed in the minds of the jurors. Carson is not one to take chances."

Chapman made one final pronouncement to the effect that he was innocent and bore a clear conscience, to which statement the gallery once again voiced its disapproval. Holmes smiled.

Closing arguments were what was to be expected: The defence assured the jury that Chapman was not guilty, while the prosecution emphasised the abundance of evidence which indicated guilt.

During a brief recess which followed the closing arguments and preceded the charge to the jury, Holmes made yet another prediction. "I must admit, Watson, that Judge Justice Grantham is a well-respected and profound jurist; however, he is not without his peccadilloes, shall we say."

"What do you mean, Holmes?"

"On past occasions, he has often come to trial with a preconceived notion of a prisoner's guilt, which he made no attempt to conceal from the jury. I believe this judicial prejudice will become evident as he delivers his summation."

Once again, Holmes proved to be an accurate seer. In reiterating much of the prosecution's contentions, the judge emphasised the fact that Klosowski was not British, which thereby pandered to the natural xenophobia of the English. Once again this was a demonstration of what is heard cannot be unheard. He singled out for thanks the chemist, William Davidson, for keeping a record of to whom he had sold the tartar emetic and Dr. Thomas Stevenson for having correctly discovered the proof of antimony poisoning. Before he instructed the jury to come to a proper conclusion in the case, he went out of his way to express the thanks of the Crown to Holmes, Abberline and myself for having efficiently and effectively pursued the investigation, without which a successful conclusion might not have been reached. At that point he addressed the twelve men good and true saying, "Gentlemen, will you consider your verdict?" The jury retired to begin their deliberations and the court recessed to await the result.

Holmes and I had barely left Courtroom Number One, exited the building and reached Bailey Street when court was called back into session with the announcement that the jury had reached a verdict. Holmes glanced at his pocket watch. "Hmm, Watson, eleven minutes. I believe that may be a new record."

Abberline had remained inside and thus had retained our seats. As soon as all were in their places and the accused returned to the dock, Judge Justice Grantham instructed the bailiff to bring the jury back into court and call the room to order. The silence was nearly smothering as the clerk of arraigns asked the jury foreman if they had reached a verdict.

"We have, sir. We find the prisoner guilty."

As Chapman fairly collapsed to his chair, Judge Justice Grantham prepared himself to pass sentence by placing the black death cap on his head. Declaring that he declined to call the accused by the English name he had assumed, he stated that the only solace he himself received was that he was able to address the man not as an Englishman but as a foreigner. That being said, he pronounced the sentence of death on Severin Klosowski.

Part III
Chapter Eight

The date for the execution was set for the 7th of April, three weeks after the trial had concluded. Over that time, the newspapers were replete with stories that trumpeted the upcoming execution of the Borough Poisoner and quite possibly Jack the Ripper. Abberline was more than willing to fan the flames of that latter supposition since that had been his contention nearly from the start. At Holmes's request, throughout all of his interviews with the press, Abberline declined to mention Holmes or myself by name. That Judge Justice Grantham had mentioned our names in court, it was an aside fit only for the court records and attracted very little attention from the fourth estate. What requests Holmes did receive for interviews, he deftly deflected towards Abberline while trivialising his own contributions.

And so it came to pass that the morning of the 7th of April found us standing to one side of the trap door in the execution shed at Wandsworth Prison, anxious for the drama to play itself out. We were told that while Klosowski – for that is the name under which he was convicted and sentenced, awaited his fate in a ten-foot square cell over the previous several weeks, he penned numerous letters to the press, which claimed his innocence and that he was an American citizen. Major Knox, the governor of the prison, made mention of the fact that Klosowski's legal wife, Lucy had arrived at the prison with her daughter, in one last attempt to persuade him to at least grant her recognition. Klosowski adamantly denied any knowledge of her and refused to even see her. Holmes stated to Major Knox that this came as no surprise to him.

"As I explained to Abberline following our interview with the accused, Chapman has entirely dissociated himself from Klosowski and anything to do with Klosowski, which certainly includes the admission that he even so much as knew Lucy Baderski, much less having been married to her and fathered her daughter. For him to do so would be a tacit admission that he is Jack the Ripper, which he will not, probably cannot, do."

"Are you saying that he is insane, Mr. Holmes?"

"Yes, I do believe he is insane, Major, criminally insane. But he is also a genius in that he has, as described by Dr. Freud and Dr. Janet, subconsciously channeled that insanity into a self-defense mechanism so complete that he truly believes that he has no association with Klosowski in any regard whatsoever. Of course, this has nothing to do with the poisonings. He simply denies having committed them, even in the face of overwhelming evidence."

"Be that as it may, Holmes," insisted Abberline, "I am adamant in my belief that in a short time we will have seen the last of Jack the Ripper."

It was only moments later that we heard a scuffling of feet as Klosowski and the execution party ascended the thirteen steps to the gallows. Half supported by the guards, Klosowski constantly muttered, as if to convince himself that his name was George Chapman. After he arrived at the trap door, his legs were strapped together and his arms bound tightly to his body. Just prior to the white hood and noose being placed over his head, Klosowski stiffened to his full height and angrily yelled, "I curse those who would take my life! My name is Chapman. I am innocent! Innocent!"

All things being in place, Mr. Billington looked toward Major Knox, who gave a nod. Mr. Billington pulled the lever and the deed was done. I feel I may speak freely as to the combined attitude of our little coterie of witnesses to the execution: It was one of quiet satisfaction. Hands were shaken all round as we expressed our thanks to Major Knox and our congratulations to Mr. Billington for an efficiently performed duty. We then exited the shed, back out into the morning's fittingly dismal weather to make our way across the prison yard, back to our carriage and thence to Baker Street.

Now, all these years later, I find that a coda may be added to the narrative. Aside from the occasional independent reprehensible act, so common in the vicinity of Whitechapel, the abominations of the Ripper have never made another appearance. Shortly after the execution, Lucy Baderski remarried to another Polish man by the name of Frank Szysmanski and disappeared quite completely from the public eye. In 1904, Abberline left the Pinkerton Detective Agency to retire to a quiet life in Bournemouth. Learning of the death of Irene Adler in October of 1903, Holmes brought his career as the world's first consulting detective to a close and retired to the bucolic life of beekeeping and study in the villa on the South Downs, Essex, which we had reconnoitered in 1902. As for myself, ever since the influenza epidemic claimed my wife in 1918, I have lived alone, save my manservant, Carstairs, at 221 Baker Street, the address which birthed so many of the adventures for Holmes and myself. I do see him occasionally, though not as often as either of us would wish, since we each manage to keep ourselves quite busy in our own separate ways.

As I pored over my notes and the newspaper clippings relating to the Whitechapel horror in preparation for the writing of this report of our involvement, I noted the absence of Holmes's name in the press. Over the years, subsequent accounts of the events have posited the theory that it was only through the guidance of Holmes that the case was solved. Not to denigrate the results of Abberline's perseverance, but it is indeed Holmes who deserves the lion's share of the credit. As for my own meagre contributions, they were likewise never mentioned in any of the articles. But that is only as it should be for a mere chronicler.

CPSIA information can be obtained
at www.ICGtesting.com
Printed in the USA
BVHW042146030423
661715BV00004B/42